MW00638013

The Brilliancy Cluster

had one very famous planet, a planet of fable that until now had been seen only once: Meirjain the Wanderer, a planet which had no sun of its own but which instead swung from star to star like an interstellar comet, weaving an apparently random path within the cluster.

The stars of Brilliancy were only light-hours apart, allowing Meirjain to steer a miraculous, sinuous course which gave it an equable climate for nearly all the time. This was taken as evidence that the Wanderer's motion was the result of artifice. It had been discovered three centuries ago. Men had landed on it, had sampled its treasures. Then it had been allowed to disappear again, melting untrackably into cluster like a molecule of sugar in colored water.

And now word had it that the Wanderer had been sighted again. And the great treasure hunt was on. . . .

Barrington J. Bayley
in DAW editions:

THE FALL OF CHRONOPOLIS
THE GRAND WHEEL
STAR WINDS
THE GARMENTS OF CAEAN
COLLISION COURSE

THE PILLARS OF ETERNITY

Barrington J. Bayley

DAW BOOKS, INC.

DONALD A. WOLLHEIM, PUBLISHER

1633 Broadway, New York, NY 10019

COPYRIGHT ©, 1982, BY BARRINGTON J. BAYLEY

All Rights Reserved.

Cover art by Wayne D. Barlowe.

FIRST PRINTING, MARCH 1982

1 2 3 4 5 6 7 8 9

DAW TRADEMARK REGISTERED
U.S. PAT. OFF. MARCA
REGISTRADA. HECHO EN U.S.A.

PRINTED IN U.S.A.

Chapter

ONE

He came slowly down the arcaded avenue that led from the landing ground. He was a blunt, stocky man encased in a modsuit, the ribbed, scruffy appearance of which might have caused some to think of him as an old trader who had grown careless about his equipment. They would have been wrong: though the modsuit was standard wear for shipkeepers, adaptable to a variety of gravities, he would have been happy to shuck it off like a torn jacket. His muscles were lithe and flexible, though now beginning to stiffen a little, for in his youth he had often scorned the use of a modsuit altogether, and he had trodden many worlds. His face was clearly unaccustomed to expressing emotion: impassive, square, pockmarked, jutting forward from the collar of the suit and surmounted by shorn grey hair. A perceptive person might have seen it as a face that masked suffering. This man, such a person might have said, has known pain, and has not overcome it. But there were unlikely to be such persons here in Hondora. A trader's town, on a planet whose culture was all borrowed from other sources, had little room for sensitivity. Here people would notice only how much he could be induced to bend in price, would ask only where he had been, where he was able to go. They would take more interest in his ship than in himself.

His ship. They would do well, he might have said to himself, to look at his ship.

Joachim Boaz was how he named himself. Captain was

how he styled himself, preferring the archaism over the more modern "shipkeeper." There was a reason for this eccentricity. He did not see himself as his ship's keeper. Quite the reverse.

The air had a balmy, lemony quality, like aerial sherbet. It was distinctive of class-C planets, and resulted from the overlarge yellow suns that abounded in the region, or more properly speaking from the mixture of secondary gases in the atmosphere, gases which such suns exuded when they expelled the material that was to form planetary systems. Captain Boaz drew the tangy breeze deep into his lungs. He cast a lingering glance at the luminous, sulfur-colored sky. He liked it here, to the extent he ever liked anything.

The arcade was fringed with fragrant tree blossoms. He pressed on, ignoring any who passed him on the avenue, and shortly came to the edge of the town. Youths and girls gazed languidly through the shaded entrances of service rooms. Stray wisps of conversation drifted to him, scarcely noticed by him but nevertheless recorded in his brain and simultaneously transmitted to his ship which stood parked a mile away. *"Choc me one more style . . ." ". . . wild one . . ." ". . . the rad gap's closed up in Ariadne now . . . can't get through . . ." ". . . have you ever killed a girl like me before? . . ."*

In the meantime his ship was transmitting subliminal signals to him, guiding him with unheard suggestions. He was prompted to enter a drum-shaped room where men in dhotis and togas sat on benches against the walls. Some drank, some sniffed yellow powder, some talked to breastless girls draped in loose shifts. Walls and ceiling were bare of ornament. They were the color of chalk, except at the rear where an ochrous red tunnel gaped, serving robots shifting from foot to foot in its mouth.

In the center of the room was a circular table occupied by five men, four of them shipkeepers, by the signs on their chests. The other was a merchant with cargoes to be moved.

Pausing, Captain Boaz waited to be noticed. Eyes swiveled, saw his modsuit, his cargo carrier's sign.

"Will you join us, shipkeeper?" called the merchant jovially. "The game is better the more the players."

Idly Boaz thought: for you it is. He took a vacant seat, and spoke in a dour tone. "I can take a load Harkio way. Nowhere else."

"Harkio?" the merchant squeaked in surprise. Boaz was breaking an unspoken rule of contract bargaining by stating his intentions at the outset like this. The other players gave him glances of disapproval.

"Yes, I might have something in that quarter," the merchant said smoothly. "Will you sit this round out, then? We'll come to it."

Boaz nodded. He took a small deck of picture cards from his pocket and began to shuffle them in an habitual, self-calming ritual. Those present would recognize the cards and know him for a colonnader.

He relaxed, inspecting a card occasionally. Games were played with such cards once. That was long ago, when a card deck could be depended on to stay inert and not play tricks at the behest of its owner.

A slot in the center of the table disgorged the card pack's equivalent: shiny cubes an inch on a side, guaranteed fully randomized by the house. The merchant was banker. He took a cube; the others each took one. They all examined the facets for the symbols that in a few moments appeared there.

Boaz ignored the proceedings and concentrated on his cards. No one seemed to know how game bargaining had begun; but shipkeepers were generally born gamblers and, after all, it was only a logical extension of haggling. The shipkeepers made bids that represented what they would be prepared to carry a cargo for. The merchant tried to drive them down by calling their bluff. In the last resort it was the cards that decided.

It could mean that a shipkeeper would have to carry a cargo for below cost. Or he could collect an exorbitant fee. Usually, however, matters worked out reasonably enough.

The merchant gave a grunt of satisfaction as he held up his cube, the signs flashing from it in pastel colors. "Excellent, Rodrige. You will be able to afford a holiday after this trip! Now, then. The ariadne gap is closed up, I hear. For the time being I shall hold my Ariadne-vectored goods in store; perhaps the gap will open up again. Now let us see . . . Harkio!" He looked up at Boaz. "Your name, shipkeeper?"

"I am Captain Joachim Boaz," Boaz said.

"Ah! How quaint! What is the load capacity of your ship?"

"Two and one-fifth milliards."

"That should suffice. Let us play."

Rodrige, who in fact had achieved a worse deal than he had hoped for, left the table with a sour face. Captain Boaz spoke again.

"I do not wish to play; I am not in the mood for it. I will take your cargo for the cost of the fuel plus a point eight percent for depreciation."

The merchant's face showed pleasure when he received this offer. The shipkeepers gave Boaz looks of malice. He was joyriding, taking a cargo simply to finance himself as a passenger on his own ship. "That might be agreeable . . . any other offers, gentlemen?"

"What could there be?" muttered one bitterly. They left, allowing Boaz to feel their dislike.

When they had gone a look of anxiety crossed the merchant's features. "Your ship . . . is it sound? I do not know you. Are you qualified?"

The barest hint of a smile almost came to Boaz. He pulled an identibloc from his pocket. The merchant's face smoothed out and became bland as he read it. "Ah yes . . . that should do . . ."

"My ship is open to your inspection."

"I will rely on your experience, good shipkeeper—or should I call you 'Captain,' eh? Ha ha! Well, then, Harkio. I have a consignment of Boems for Schloss III."

"Boems?" said Boaz.

"Something wrong, Captain?" the merchant inquired.

A moral struggle ensued within Captain Boaz. He had always refused to take Boems before. Some philosophers classed them as sentient beings. In which case to traffic in them would involve him in slavery.

"I am not sure I can do it."

"What? Ah, I see your problem. You are a colonnader, are you not? You follow an ethical code. Luckily I am a skeptic in gnostical matters. Well, you need not worry. These Boems have no conscious process. It has been scrambled out of them, if any ever existed. They would classify as corpses."

"Then what use are they?"

"Oh, they can perform many functions of the simpler sort," explained the merchant in good humor. "They are used mainly in children's toys. Does that clear it up for you?"

Boaz decided. He was keen to get to Harkio.

"It's agreed."

"Good. Now let me see—hmm, hmm." The merchant was computing the figures with his adp implant. "The Boems amass one point seven eight milliards. What's the mass of your ship?"

Boaz told him. The merchant worked out how many fuel sticks the trip would need, added a little leeway, reckoned the cost plus Boaz's depreciation.

"Two hundred and twenty-eight point one eight nine psalters," he muttered. Captain Boaz nodded, having simultaneously done the same calculation on his own adplant. The merchant wrote out a contract on a vissheet, finishing with a flourish. Each touched it to his forehead, recording his body odor as a signature of compliance with the terms. The merchant counted out some dominolike coins from a bag on his lap, giving them to Boaz wrapped in a cloth.

"Here you are, then. My goods will be delivered tomorrow morning."

He left, looking satisfied. For a while Captain Boaz sat alone at the table, the folded cloth of money in his hand, watching the fizzy sunshine filter through the open doorway.

A nymphgirl who had been drinking on a side bench stood up suddenly, discarded her shift and began to dance naked. Her body was hairless, narrow-waisted and without breasts. She was just like a girl child enlarged to the size of a full-grown woman. It was the current fashion in Hondora, again a fashion imported from nearby worlds.

The girl stopped dancing when a robot stepped quietly from the red tunnel to place a hand on her shoulder. "You must not do that here, madam. This is a place of business. For that, you must go to other establishments."

Wordlessly she picked up her shift. Glancing scornfully around her, she stalked out.

Captain Boaz rose to address the robot. "Where can I get ship fuel?"

"The nearest stockist is close by, sir," the robot said, turning its smooth face toward him. "Proceed down the avenue and take the second turning on the right. Proceed farther a hundred yards. The stockist's name is Samsam."

Boaz quit the room and again walked the arcade, going deeper into Hondora. Farther down, the avenue became more lively, assailing him with motley smells and noises. Metal clashing, food frying, the aromas of a hundred mingled drugs and perfumes. He heard laughter, screams of mirth, the tinkling sounds of soft music. Men and nymphgirls spilled out of doorless openings and chased one another, kicking up the orange dust of the unpaved concourse.

Under shimmering awnings merchandise was displayed on glittering trays: foods, sweetmeats, drugs, trinkets, garments, a thousand intricate artifacts. Captain Boaz's step faltered. He had come to a stall offering Boems for sale. The pale micelike slabs were piled carelessly in the trays, their crystalline ridges jammed into one another.

Were they decerebrated or not? Captain Boaz looked away and strode on.

The side street was quieter. Samsam's was an unprepossessing shop without windows or display stall. Inside it was dim and cool.

The shopkeeper shuffled out from the back, blinking. "Yes?"

"Good day." Captain Boaz presented his credentials and placed the money on the counter. "I need fuel sticks. I'm told you charge standard price, otherwise I'll go elsewhere."

"Oh, yes indeed."

The old man leaned across the counter, and his voice fell. "I can get you some for less, if you like."

"Thank you, no. I want no stolen merchandise, and no inferior fuel. Give me good rods."

The shopkeeper turned to the shelves behind the counter that were stacked with sticks. "What size?"

"X20. Give me five full-length, and one you'll have to cut."

"What d'you want it cut to, then?" The man selected sticks and laid them on the counter.

"Give me thirty-seven over a hundred," Boaz said, stating a fraction.

"Oh, I don't cut to anything less than an inch," the shopkeeper grumbled. "I can't get rid of scraps like that."

"Very well, give me four over ten," Boaz said impatiently. The man picked up a stick and took it to a cutting machine at the end of the counter. He put it in the grip, calibrated it, and set the blade to whining at high speed through the yellow rod.

While this happened Boaz picked up another of the rods and ran his eye along it as if testing the straightness of an arrow. It was about two feet long and two inches in diameter. It sparkled like sugar frosting and was rough to the touch.

The special kind of energy that resided in the rods was put there by a very expensive process. Each one would carry two milliards of shipweight a distance of ten light-years. Boaz unfolded the cloth that contained his money and counted out rectangular coins while the shopkeeper placed the sticks in a carrying bag. He received the change, thanked the vendor and stepped back out into the lemon sunshine.

Halfway down the side street, his ship told him he was being stalked. He tucked the fuel sticks under his arm. It was those they were after. About a minute later, his ship reported the attack was imminent.

Then a spring lasso snaked out from the nearby wall, jerking him off balance. Like a paper box, a section of wall folded in and revealed a narrow alley, and in it two men, one wielding the lasso and hauling Boaz inward, the other shifting from foot to foot with hands reaching out, like a wrestler looking for a hold.

For a moment Boaz could not deploy his strength. Still clutching the fuel sticks, he was dragged into the alley. Only then was he able to grab the lasso with his free hand, seizing it by the haft and pulling the man down on top of him.

For a stocky, modsuited man, his subsequent speed was

a surprise to his attackers. He rolled, and was on his feet, in almost the same movement delivering a kick to the lasso man's coccyx, snapping his spine.

The man gave a bubbling moan, face down and moving his arms like a crippled insect. He would not live long. Boaz turned to face the second robber over the semi-paralyzed form of his comrade. The man had a gun. Boaz saw a snarl of fear, felt heat as the beam struck his chest.

But this sensation was measured in microseconds. Two miles away on the landing ground Boaz's ship was responding to the events impinging on his body. Billions upon billions of digital pulses passed down the tight directional beam it maintained, and set about arranging his body's defenses. The lethal shot from the thief's gun was diverted, dissipated in a thin blaze of light.

Taking one step forward with the fuel sticks still under his arm, Captain Boaz tore the gun from the mugger's grasp, smashing its handle against the wall so that the charge pack broke open and tossing it aside. The thief backed away with a glance to his rear. The alley was a dead end, probably constructed specifically for the purpose of robbers.

"We weren't going to hurt you, shipkeeper," he pleaded quickly. "We only wanted your fuel sticks."

"Liar. That was a kill shot."

"Look what you did to my friend—"

He could not evade Boaz, who grabbed him by the front of his toga and forced him to his knees, still using only one hand. Then he took him by the throat.

Just as Boaz began to throttle him, a transformation came over the thief's face. His terror dissolved into a dreamy leer, and he looked up at Boaz.

"You goin' to kill me?" he asked breathlessly.

Boaz glanced at the still moaning form behind him. Abruptly he saw his posture in a new light, and he did not like it. He withdrew his hand. The robber sagged, looked relieved, disappointed, edgy.

No expression at all showed on Boaz's face. He backed out of the alley, turned, and set off for the main avenue.

He came again to the ship ground. A few dozen ships dotted the flat, three-mile-square expanse. They loomed

and seemed to drift on the hazy air. A few were halfheart-
edly streamlined for a swift getaway, but most ship design-
ers did not consider the small saving in fuel worth the
trouble and ungainly shapes abounded.

Evening was coming on. The sun was low and on the
sky's opposite horizon a few stars showed. Overhead was
an unusual sight; this system was irregular in its planetary
formation, and the planet was actually the binary satellite
of a gas giant. It could be seen glowing palely in the effer-
vescent sky, its rings clearly visible.

The ship ground was a raised plateau. From its vantage
the landscape and the town were laid out like a map. Captain Boaz paused to look at it. Why was it, he wondered,
that on nearly all man-inhabited worlds he had visited he
received this same feeling of universe old and in decline?
A universe experiencing a soft autumn, wearing out, losing
vitality. Could the universe really be approaching its end,
when it would dissolve in mind-fire? Or was it only human
society that exuded such decay?

He reminded himself that the impression could not be
other than subjective: it emanated from his own feelings.
Such a belief had arisen before, when in fact mankind had
been very young, as he knew from reading the works of
philosophers and historians such as Plutarch, Lucretius
and Marcus Aurelius, who had lived before there was even
a machine civilization. They too had concluded, for reasons that seemed trivial now, that the world was in its
dotage, and they, it was evident, had stood on some hill as
Boaz did now, and saw the fey melancholy that seemed
to invest everything and even to drift down from the stars.

It said something for Captain Boaz's character that he
could muse in so pensive a manner just after having killed
one man, barely refraining from killing another. It was not
that he was a cruel or heartless man; on the contrary his
adherence to colonnade philosophy gave him a strictly ethical outlook. But, in comparison with what he had known,
it simply did not seem important. They had come against
him, and that was that.

A flowing tread-rail carried him up the ship's side to the
manport. Inside, he went to the engine cabin, where he
busied himself with checking out the fuel sticks, measuring
their straightness (vital for smooth performance) and sam-

pling their peculiar energy, which alone could send a ship faster than light. Finally he slammed them into the empty induction tubes (on landing there had been less than an inch of stick left).

He went to the main cabin and prepared himself a simple meal of the special foods he ate. He felt at home. The metal, the processors, the adp, the transmitters, enwrapped him. He was inside his ship like a babe inside the womb. No longer did it need to protect him from afar; there was no fear of distance, no narrow control beam. Its emanations regulated his nervous system, his perceptions, carefully preserved him from harm, and did it all by means of a suffused ambiance of constant signaling that filled the air around him.

His ship; it was his tragedy, and his salvation, and his hope. It reached out its gentle hands and maintained him for as long as he remained within range. It gave him abnormal strength and immunity from many weapons. At ten miles its efficacy began to fade and he would fall ill. At fifteen miles he would die, in a horrible agony that was a repetition of the agony he could remember.

And the ship, just as it could reach out to regulate his ravaged body, could also reach out with its subtle beams to tell him what was happening elsewhere. Boaz settled himself in a low armchair, and without really meaning to, found himself indulging in the random spying he would sometimes resort to as a means of diverting his mind from the broodings that threatened to overwhelm him. His mind seemed to drift, as if in a waking dream, through the streets and buildings of Hondora. The sun was down; the day's business was over. The town was giving itself over to the pursuits that mainly interested its inhabitants: the pursuits of aimless pleasure.

The ship's beams lunged softly, undetectably, through metal, through walls of lithoplaster, paint and HCferric. Boaz perceived the interior of a crowded bar. Nymphgirls danced in the center of the room, rarely with men, who held back and drank solidly.

His perspective shifted, zoomed in on a booth at the far end. A tough-looking man sat at a narrow table, a tankard in front of him. His face was broad and flat, with a spade jaw, squashed nose and widely separated eyes, as if it had been hit with a mallet. Sharing the table with him was a girl with long red hair, red lips, long cheeks. Her movements were mobile; she gestured and shifted as she talked, quite unlike her stolid partner.

There had been tease-play between them. Boaz saw that they had only met that night, but she was seeking a relationship. He was less enthusiastic, offhanded but not dismissive. Consequently they needled one another.

He looked at her in annoyance. "I keep thinking I've met you before. I have, haven't I?"

"Have you?"

"Ah, I don' know." He drawled his words, scarcely moved his jaw when he spoke. "Maybe it was your sister. You got a sister?"

"Maybe."

"Yah—I guess it was somebody else. There are a million girls like you. I've had a hundred, at least."

She leaned close, looked up at him from under long lashes. Her mouth hung open lasciviously. "You ever kill a girl like me?"

"I've killed lots of girls."

Boaz became sleepy. He dozed. The man and the girl danced, drank, drifted in and out of his awareness. There was a certain savage intensity developing between them. When he came fully awake again they were in a private room, facing one another across the mattressed floor like animals ready to pounce on one another. Both were naked.

Suddenly her eyes hardened. "You *have* killed somebody like me before. I'm Jodie. Remember?"

He looked uncertain, flexing his muscled body in impatience. "Jodie? But your face. It's not the same. Not quite, anyway."

She looked triumphant. "I'm altered. A hormonal imbalance in the tank. Too much thyroid. But I'm Jodie all right—and I remember." Her voice became fervid. "*God, how I remember!*"

With a darting movement she bent to her discarded clothing and came up with a coiled tendril of an object. It was a parawhip. Her hair swung about her shoulders as she straightened. Her words came in gasps. "I've got kinky thinking about it. But this time it's going to be different. This time, *I'm going to kill you!*"

The whip sang out to reach for the man's nerves and incapacitate him for her pleasure. But he was too quick for her. He sidestepped. Then he sprang, caught her wrist and twisted her arm, catching the handle of the whip with his other hand as it fell from her grasp.

"Sorry, honey, I don't go for that clone stuff." His voice was gruff and hot. "There's only one way I want to stay alive. For *you*, though——"

His big hand around her throat, he forced her to the floor. Boaz signaled the ship to withdraw from the scene. His *voyeurism* drew the line at sex murder; he found it distasteful.

The girl had a clone body stashed away somewhere. A transmitter was in her brain, something like the one in Boaz's ship, but much, much simpler. Moment by moment it fed her experiences into the sleeping clone. When she died the clone would wake up. It would have all her memories, including the memory of dying. Jodie resurrected.

Sex killing had become a fashionable cult among the sated pleasure-seekers of this region, who found through it the acme of a connection long known to psychologists: the connection between sex and death. They said there was no ecstasy to match it, because there was nothing fake about it. The original *did* die, genuinely, forever. The sense of continuity belonged only to the new, awakened clone.

At least that was what most people thought. Boaz wasn't so sure. He believed that there was such a thing as the soul, and that it was not spatially limited. Perhaps it followed along with the identical memory. Just the same, he did not like the death cult. The clone's memory of sex death caused it to seek the same experience over again. It was a vicious circle of perversion.

Boaz himself had no clone body. He would have welcomed death if it could have helped him. But it could not help him. It would still leave the past, where his agony lay.

He slept, still slumped in the armchair. After ten hours he awoke to find the merchant's trucks arriving. Even before he roused himself his ship robots had put out a derrick and were clambering down the side of the hull. He followed, and watched them hoist the crates into the hold.

He opened the last crate. Inside were Boems, from a unique planet where crystalline growths proliferated to a fantastic degree. Boems were simply the most advanced form of this growth. Whether they were simply natural crystals with a better than adp complexity or evolved living forms, sentient but non-motile, had never been established. One could converse with them, using the right kind of modem, but the responses could as equally be a processing of the inquirer's own information as genuine.

Whatever the truth, they made useful control systems. Put a Boem in a cybernetic device and it became almost a person—hence the attraction for the toy industry, even for those cerebrally scrambled. Manufactured adp, on the other hand, lacked spontaneity.

Boaz had no way of knowing whether these were in fact scrambled, as the merchant had promised, but it was far too late for him to be able to reconsider the contract. He would have to deliver the cargo before attending to any quest of his own. Such was the law.

He put his odor to the delivery note. The trucks rolled away, the robots climbed back inside, the derrick withdrew. Captain Boaz mounted the tread-rail and took himself to the flight cabin. The first of the fuel sticks was sparked and began to deliver its energy. Slowly, the cargo carrier rose through the lemon-colored sky.

Chapter

TWO

Once Boaz was among the blazing lights that were stars and the curtains of splendor that were stretches of dust and gas, there was nothing to distract him. As his ship sped through the galactic realm he had little to do but sit, and as he sat he brooded, and when he brooded the past could not help but well up. Onplanet he could always direct his attention elsewhere. But here there was only the ship and the void.

The faint drone of the ship engine was a constant background. His attention, even when resisting at first, found itself flicking from one to another of the images that bubbled up to claim it.

Memory took over.

Captain Joachim Boaz had not always borne that name. His original name had been a single word, a curse, a nickname, a word he would not bother to articulate now; it did not seem like him anymore. Born in the warrens of Corsair, he had never known a father and saw little of his mother. From the age of ten he had been alone, trying to join one of the conduit gangs, as the packs of juveniles who terrorized the warrens were called.

But Boaz was ill-fated from birth. He was born deformed, his spine twisted, his limbs warped, unable to walk but only to hump himself along with a stout stick he held in both hands, and which was also his defense against the kicks and blows he received from young and old alike.

He never was accepted by any gang, though he ran with any that would tolerate him, able to get up a fair speed as he lolloped along with his stick.

Unable to share in the thievery and robbery by which the conduit gangs survived, he spent much of his time begging at the spaceport. By the time he was fifteen he had conceived an ambition: he wanted to be a shipkeeper. Those straight-backed, steady-eyed men, owners of their own ships, able to go anywhere, were heroes to him as they strode about the spaceground. They were less liable to kick him aside with a well-shod boot than were space passengers, mechanics or even company crewmen; more inclined to give him a coin instead. Dimly Boaz guessed that there was more to the universe than Corsair's brutish, pitiless society. When he saw a ship soar up into the blue (Corsair had a blue sky) he thought of escape.

When he was sixteen, it happened. Boaz came humping out of the conduit onto a shadowed corner of the spaceground. Half a dozen Slashers, the conduit gang he avoided most, were chasing him, shouting his name at him, the name he hated, the name that described what he was.

He might even have got away from them had not a pylon been in his way. With his mode of locomotion he could not change direction easily at speed. It gave one of them a chance to head him off. His stick was kicked from under him and went skittering away. He scrabbled after it, but they had him now. They put a prong on him to hear him scream.

He only felt one jolt. Then a change came over the scene. The Slashers paused, their yells cut short. The prong was suspended in midair. Boaz raised his eyes as he lay on the floor of the spaceground. He saw a pair of bare feet, above them bare ankles and legs bare up to the mid-thigh. Then the hem of a chiton, a togalike garment that draped loosely from the shoulders.

It was a garment worn by professional people who did not have to work much. The young Boaz peered up over his humped, twisted shoulder. Above the white fabric of the chiton he saw blue eyes gazing from a clean-shaven face with hair cut neatly across the forehead.

The stranger must have stepped from behind the pylon.

The Slashers could have dealt with him easily, but they seemed too surprised to act for the moment. The conduit gangs had a tacit agreement with the port managers: they did not molest off-world visitors on the spaceground itself. Yet that did not seem to be all that was restraining them. There was something in the unflinching look of the newcomer that was overpowering.

He made a sweeping gesture with his arm. "Be off with you."

They did not move at once but after a few moments, with surly glances, they made their way back to the conduit. The stranger retrieved Boaz's stick and handed it to him. Boaz planted its end on the floor and hauled himself up it until he was as nearly upright as he could be. He came not far above the stranger's waist.

"Thank you, sir. If you could spare a small coin, sir . . ."

The man in the chiton ignored his automatically replayed spiel. He was looking Boaz over with a professional eye.

"Were you born in that condition, young man?"

Nervously Boaz took one hand off his stick to clutch his ragged tunic protectively to him, bunching it up at his throat. "Yes, sir," he whispered.

"Have you ever seen a doctor?"

"A doctor, sir?"

Boaz scarcely knew what a doctor was. Sickness on Corsair was as rare as congenital disorder; natural selection had bred it out.

"A doctor is someone who mends a body that has gone wrong." The man spoke patiently, at once understanding the extent of Boaz's ignorance.

"No, sir." Boaz held out his hand but then, perceiving that he was to be given nothing, made as if to shuffle off.

"Wait," the man said. "I wish to talk to you. Follow me."

Wonderingly Boaz obeyed. He felt peculiar and out of place as the man escorted him into one of the hotels lining the spaceground. Soon he found himself in a well-lit, well-furnished room. It was all strange to him; he was not used to furnished interiors.

The man spoke, but not to Boaz. A minute later a servitor appeared and delivered a covered tray. Inside it was an oval plate of spiced food. The man invited Boaz to eat.

The food was delicious, but scant in quantity. Boaz did not guess that this was because his host, seeing his half-starved features, did not wish to overburden his stomach. With it was a fizzy drink, the sort Boaz liked and bought often. He gulped it greedily.

The man in the chiton let him finish before beginning to talk to him again. "Your body can be mended," he told him. "Your bones can be remade and straightened. Your tissues can be stimulated and adjusted, so that you will attain your proper growth. Did you not know this?"

Boaz shook his head. He had never even thought about it.

"The process is, of course, very costly."

The stranger was making some sort of pitch, that much Boaz knew very well. But what it was he could want from him was a total mystery. He listened while the man continued in his mild, factual voice. He could see to it that Boaz got the required treatment, he said. He was prepared to take Boaz off Corsair and to a planet where friends of his, skilled doctors, would straighten out his body. But he was not making this offer only to help Boaz. There was something he wanted out of it, too—something that could be greatly to Boaz's advantage if all went well. If not—well, the risk was a small one, it was unlikely that anything would go wrong that could not be put right. At the worst the experiment would fail, but they would still ensure that Boaz ended up with good bones. He promised Boaz that.

The price Boaz had to pay for these benefits was that he was to be used as an experimental subject. In fact, the orthopedic surgeons—bonemakers, the man called them—would replace Boaz's entire skeleton. In place of his poor twisted bones, they would insert bones they had made themselves. These would be as good as natural bones in strength and durability, and they would contain marrow for making blood. But they would have a lot of silicon in them. Every gram of this silicon would comprise adp.

"Do you know what adp is?" the man asked him.

Boaz shook his head. The man shrugged. "Automatic data processing. It is what all machines work by. The servitor that brought you your meal. Every type of control system." He tapped his brow. "The implant in my skull that allows me to calculate beyond limit. In effect, your whole skeleton will consist of microprocessing. It will be like a second person within you, with new perceptions, new feelings, new abilities. Except that there will be no second person there. These benefits will be all yours, whenever you wish to make use of them.

"This is the natural direction for human evolution to take. The brain is not large enough, even with adplants added. Silicon bones provide the room for extra processes, while still doubling as a skeleton. So far the technique has been developed using animals . . . the vital stage of adaptation to human beings has been delayed while we waited for one of us to volunteer as a subject . . . You, however, could solve our little problem. You are unusual; there are not many congenitally deformed people in the galaxy."

"Why'd you come to Corsair looking for someone like me? 'Cause there are no doctors here?"

"I did not come to Corsair looking for anything. This spaceport is a stopover point; I shall be here for a few hours waiting for my connection to Aurelius. It is by simple good fortune that I found you—good fortune for us both, I hope."

Later, Boaz was to compare these silicon bones with the Boems, the crystalline adp that grew naturally. It had made him think that perhaps Boems weren't sentient after all, any more than the bones were.

The sixteen-year-old beggar boy had not understood everything the bonemaker said to him. Later he was to find that fullness of explanation was an ethical consideration on the other's part. To estimate another's level of comprehension was arrogance, since it was nearly always to underestimate his mental capacity. Civilized standards required that all the facts be made available for the listener to understand or not, as the case may be.

In fact, the bonemaker's talk of new perceptions went right over Boaz's head. But he understood clearly that the stranger was offering to take him off Corsair, and besides that was offering him hope of a kind he had never dared to contemplate.

But why should he trust this chiton-wearing offworlder,

a man whose class was despised in the warrens because of the ease and comfort of its life-style? Boaz had a reason, which he could not articulate but which told on him as he sat across from his host. All the man's words and actions were careful and deliberate, yet they displayed no desire to impress. He had not once smiled at Boaz. He had not tried to apply persuasion. He had put facts, and had left it to Boaz to decide. It was the first time in his life that Boaz had been treated as an equal.

He decided.

"I'll come with you," he said

The bonemaker's name was Hyton. When asked his, the boy simply went even paler than usual and looked away. Hyton did not inquire again; and Boaz found that he could manage without a name. In a week they were on Aurelius, and here his horizons expanded swiftly.

His first change of perspective came almost immediately. He was confused by the unfailing courtesy shown him by the men into whose charge he had delivered himself. When the time came for physical examination, he flinched as they approached him, and could barely refrain from cowering.

The specialist (it was another, not Hyton) team leader smiled. "There was once a civilization, you know," he said to Boaz, "in which a malformed person was not at all an object of contempt. Rather, he was pitied, and given special deference."

Boaz gaped.

"Matters are different now, of course. I have no doubt you have been abused a great deal."

He nodded, as though the silent youth had given him some answer. "Nature has taken over. Compassion is to some extent artificial, a product of urban life. It is more normal for a malformed specimen to be attacked and driven out by the community. That is how it is with animals, and so it is with the village mentality into which most of civilization has declined."

"And what of you?" Boaz challenged.

Again the bonemaker smiled. "We are what are known as 'colonnaders,' " he replied.

Boaz had never heard of colonnade philosophy, and this

news meant nothing to him. But it was important, he was told, that he should be instructed in it. Silicon bones were intended for people of philosophic attainment, and it was necessary to test out their effects as completely as possible.

Aurelius was in fact the planet from which colonnade philosophy had emanated. After examining him, the bone-makers proclaimed that lengthy preparation would be needed before the final operation. Suitable bones would have to be manufactured to his dimensions, and besides there was much in his musculature to be rectified. Meantime they carried out some temporary corrective work. Boaz could now walk with a limp, again with the help of a stick, though his leg muscles were assisted by calipers and fired by adplants.

Hyton took him to Theta, the city in the equatorial sun-belt which was the home of colonnade thought. Colonnaders did not, in fact, call themselves colonnaders at all. The word was a popularism, coined from Theta's distinctive architectural feature—its immensely long and spacious colonnades and peristyles which made the flower-decked city so delightful. To themselves, the colonnaders were merely philosophers—"lovers of wisdom."

Along these airy pathways Boaz learned the refined pleasure of cool discourse. Aurelius was yet another class-C planet: another with a lemon sherbet sky, investing the colonnades with a crocus-colored radiance, as though the stone itself were soaked in saffron. Gazing down the endless perspectives was like staring into a benign infinity, while unfamiliar and marvelous ideas suffused Boaz's brain.

Hyton introduced him to a man called Madrigo, whom he was eventually to look upon as his mentor. Madrigo paid no attention to his lack of experience in the world; he informed him from the start that this was of no moment. At first Boaz was inclined, more or less by a reflex learned on Corsair, to seek small advantages for himself, even to try to manipulate those around him. But this quickly faded when it met with no response.

Instead he began to emulate the behavior of the people around him: the dispassionate considerateness, the assumption of good will on the part of others—for all conscious beings, Madrigo assured him, were in reality common citizens of a single city, the city of the universe.

But most important of all was the attitude Madrigo taught him to adopt toward himself. The mental condition striven for by colonnader training was known as ataraxy; undisturbed consciousness, or stoical indifference to events.

"Everything is transitory, everything is arbitrary, yet at the same time everything is inevitable," Madrigo told him. "Whatever happens to you must be borne, without resentment if bad, without glee if good. Your own unconditioned consciousness is the secret of life."

"You can't help your feelings," Boaz mumbled.

"That is why you are here. You will learn to recognize your feelings, and not to be ruled by them. It will come."

And he *did* learn. Guided by Madrigo, he made what was to him an amazing discovery: that his own feelings were *not* the most important things in the world, not even to himself. He learned to detach himself from troublesome emotions, to treat them as objects external to himself. When he did this, he found that his senses grew a little sharper, his attention span a little longer. Gradually, too, he found that behind the cruder kind of emotions, based on desire or the thwarting of it, were feelings of a broader sort—warmth toward others, pleasure that was softer, more voluptuous. These, too, Madrigo warned him, he must not become attached to. He must always remember that the world was, in a sense, illusory.

Boaz balked at this. "It seems pretty real to me," he sniffed.

"So it is; it is real, but it is not self-sustaining. Everything that happens passes, and fades, and so it is as if it had never been—until it happens again."

Boaz did not understand what Madrigo meant by these last words until, some time later, he came to know something of colonnader cosmology. The world consisted in reality of *mind-fire*, their term for a kind of undifferentiated consciousness. Something happened in this mind-fire; it began to attenuate here and thicken there, becoming uneven. From this movement there began to differentiate out the physical elements. The sidereal universe evolved, and the elements combined in countless ways. Yet mind-fire was always there, even if reduced in quantity and quality, and it coarsened itself sufficiently to become *individual* consciousness, manifest in organic creatures.

This was how the universe came into being, congealed, as it were, out of mind-fire. But only for a period. After an unknown number of billions of years it entered a phase of collapse until eventually it was consumed by fire—mind-fire, the purest form of fire imaginable. The elements dissolved into it, sinking back to the latent state. Thus the world came to an end. But not forever. After a similarly protracted period of time the process began again, *exactly as before.* The manifest universe reemerged just as it had already been. Every atom, every individual, every event recurred, identical in every detail. Nothing ever changed, from eternity to eternity.

The cosmic oscillation was fundamental: two pillars of universal stability. Indeed they were but the first instance of the basic law of polarity on which all manifest existence depended.

Fond of symbolism, the colonnaders represented this law in terms of two upright pillars, one positive, one negative. And there were names for them dating back to ancient lore: *Joachim* and *Boaz.*

The crippled lad found these conceptions awesome. On a more personal level they solved a problem for him. Since coming to Theta he had given thought to the choosing of a new name for himself. The trouble was that all names he heard sounded like someone else, not himself. But now, ignoring any possible accusation of false grandeur, he decided to give himself names representative of his rebirth as a person, and besides that indicative of the new mental horizons opening before him.

He named himself *Joachim Boaz.*

His old life was finished, and he put all thought of Corsair behind. Three months later, the bonemakers announced that they were ready to perform the operation.

His heart beating (he was not yet so trained in ataraxy that he did not feel prey to fear), he submitted himself to pre-med. His body was purged of poisons and waste matter. He was meticulously cleaned and shaved. It was explained to him that he would be unconscious for ten weeks. After the skeleton replacement, he would lie in a tank where his muscles would be coaxed into adjusting themselves to his new, straightened frame. There would be a subsequent operation in which the new bones would be connected up to his nervous system. Finally, completely healed, he would be taken from the tank and allowed a further short term of recuperation. Only then would his higher brain functions be switched back on. He would awaken between crisp sheets in a fresh room with the scent of flowers wafting through an open window, and he would be new.

And so it was.

Boaz stirred in his chair. He thought he had fallen asleep and had been dreaming, but no, he was only remembering. There was a remedy for memory. It could be selectively excised by surgery or by electrical manipulation of the brain's storage areas. New memories could be introduced, even. One could have a new past, become a new, different person with different experiences. There were cults that practiced this rewriting of past life. But Boaz, a man of rigid personal integrity, had never even considered it. Life was real, and only memories that were based on real episodes counted. To accept other memories was to live in a dream, and from a dream, even if it took half of eternity, one must eventually awaken. . . .

The thought evoked a painful emotion in him, and in response the ship stirred. It was always busy, always worrying both over itself and over Boaz—they both were its province. He heard a faint hum, a click, the quietest whisper of some change of state taking place in the ever-watchful mechanisms. Then he sank into the vivid hallucinatory quality of his memories again. . . .

There was no mirror in the recuperation center. He asked for one, but they told him to be patient. First he had to learn to balance, to walk, to get used to himself. What of the bone functions? he asked. They were not switched on. He would be shown how later.

Just by looking down at himself he could see he was differently shaped. Looking around him, he could see he stood in a different relationship to his environment. No longer was his form a cowering one. He was tall: nearly as tall as most people. His spine was erect. His limbs moved freely.

His musculature was marvelously flexible and strong. It was a new, delightful experience to be able to poise his body on one foot, to stride across a room, to bend and reach out without danger of falling over. But it was remarkable how quickly he adjusted to his new condition. To his surprise, it was no longer new after a day or two; it was normal.

Only then did they bring in mirrors.

After a week they took him back to the operating theatre and put him to sleep to check out his bones on the mass of testing equipment they had there. It was like switching on a new kind of engine; if it didn't run right, there could be damage.

He woke up back in the recuperation center. Hyton was there to greet him. Everything was in order. The switching on could begin.

It was something he had to do himself, but he had to be shown how, and it was necessary to be cautious. In all, the bones had eight functions; but for the present he was to be shown only the preservation function and the felicity function, and the latter he would only be shown how to raise to Grade Three on a scale of ten.

The preservation function was simple off/on. It was, however, the only function intended to be left permanently on, and it was, moreover, the greatest triumph of the bone-maker's art so far. By supplementing the natural repair systems, it endowed the physical organism with an unprecedented ability to withstand shock and injury, even rendering organs capable of regenerating themselves to some extent, after the manner of the liver (previously the only organ able to do so). It prolonged life, slowing the biological clock.

The felicity function was of a psychological type. It engendered a state that could also be obtained—but temporarily—through the use of drugs, and which was faintly foreshadowed in the side effects of the mental exercises Boaz had received from Madrigo. Like them, the function worked on the feelings. Hyton also referred to it as "the joy function."

Its action was to open a direct conduit between sensory perception and emotional life. The sight of any scene or object, the hearing of any sound, was greeted with feelings of joy, wonderment, pleasure, happiness. Nothing was bland or mundane. The universe came to life: it glowed with radiance and meaning, from every drop of water to every spacious landscape.

The felicity function was, as Hyton had promised, like possessing another mode of perception. Boaz chuckled with delight as he gazed around him at setting two. The even, light tangerine color of the wall—how hopeful, how genial it was! The flashing mirror, with its surround of sheened bluemetal—why, it struck him at once with its sense of self-confidence, its ability to return and project images of any hue! It warmed his heart to see it!

And when he looked out of the window at the garden beyond and at the daffodil sun low in the sky—the ravishing scene made his heart burst with happiness. Just to know that all this *existed!*

"May I raise to setting three?" he asked.

"Very well, but be careful."

Switching was accomplished by means of mentally intoned syllables. So far, Boaz had been told six—two on/off pairs and the two additional settings for felicity. In his mind he spoke the syllable for the third setting—and immediately gasped at the shock-flood of emotion that the glowing, blazing scene before his eyes evoked in him. Hastily he reverted to setting two.

"You must raise any function only to the level that your consciousness is able to handle," Hyton warned him. "The danger with silicon bones is of being swamped, even eradicated, by the strength of some of the functions. Generally speaking we shall install bones only in people who have had philosophical training."

Boaz switched off felicity and came down to ground level. "What are the other functions?"

Hyton smiled. "There is adjusted chronaxy, which alters the minimum duration of nervous excitability and therefore controls the time sense by lengthening or shortening the specious present. There is also adjusted rheobase, which alters the galvanic threshold of nervous excitability; this heightens or lowers the intensity of sensory impressions. By the same token adjusted rheobase should affect the range of mental associations, provoking new chains of thought—as to that, we shall see." He paused before continuing. "There is also a sexually oriented function which I will not go into now. Then there is the kinesthetic function which makes one more alert to movement and the shapes of edges much as certain predatory animals are; dances should prove particularly entertaining when viewed with this function. . . ."

Hyton chattered on, but Boaz understood scarcely a word of what he was saying. "Why isn't there an ataraxy function?" he asked.

"Ataraxy is not a function," Hyton told him. "It is a primary condition. You have eight-function bones; they are experimental to a degree. Later models may have more functions, but ataraxy will not be one of them. Nor can it be."

Hyton paused again. "That is why you must be introduced gradually to the effects of these functions. They are designed to be used in a condition of high ataraxy, or your mind could be blown. For that reason fail-safe fuses are installed, but just the same . . . we estimate that your functions should be switched on gradually over a period of years."

"Years?" the young Boaz said. He sounded alarmed. "How many *years* am I supposed to stay here?"

There was nothing they could do to hold him, short of unethical imprisonment. All his early years his true character, cowed and beaten, had been given no chance to express itself. Now he was freed of the harshness of Corsair; his true nature was beginning to show, and it turned out that his character was an impetuous one. He yearned to roam, and his restlessness became a knot of frustration that could not tolerate any restraint.

He stuck it out for two months, during which time he learned to handle the felicity function up to setting four. Then he announced that he was going.

Hyton tried to persuade him against it; Madrigo made no attempt to do so. Boaz was adamant. He was eager to experience life; the remaining control syllables could wait until he was ready. He promised only that while he was away he would strive at all times for ataraxy, and that he would return so that the experiment could continue.

He went. And he did the bonemakers a great service.

He found out their basic mistake.

To own his own ship was still his goal, but for that he would need extensive financial credit. Meantime he entered the cargo trade as a hired hand, serving first on a cheap tatty scow with her tubes half rotted, then working his way up to the larger lines. He *did* gain experience of life, on a score of worlds, and the galaxy was as colorful as anything he could have imagined. . . .

Sometimes he would feel sorry for his tormentors back on Corsair. They, like him, would be grown men and women now, but it was unlikely that many of them would have gotten offplanet. To imagine their no doubt drear lives gave him a feeling of vengeful satisfaction that only his philosophical training prevented him from reveling in. . . .

He kept his promise. As the years passed, he did go back to Aurelius, several times, and spent months at a time there. Mostly, though, it was Madrigo who gave him his attention. The bonemakers, disappointed at not finding him permanently at their disposal, had located new, more cooperative subjects. Hyton himself, in fact, had been installed with silicon bones, and the number of bonemen and bonewomen was increasing. Still, Boaz could boast of being the first. They checked him out, debriefed him, gave him a few more syllables, the first settings of other functions. Meantime, Boaz saved as hard as he could. . . .

No longer so young, he grew mature. . . .

. . . day 29, month 3, year 716 standard time. . . .

H819 was an anamolous planet. It was lifeless, but it had a breathable atmosphere, if you didn't mind breathing in sulphides along with it or else wore an air filter. The oxygen was belched out by numerous volcanoes whose intense heat apparently split some underground oxide such as water. Boaz arrived there as a crewman on a ship bringing equipment to an alchemical research station. The company he worked for had decided to switch him to another ship, so he was left onplanet to wait for his new berth to pick him up.

He remembered craggy cliffs and burning cones, nothing moving except the constant movement of rocks dislodged by frequent ground tremors. . . .

Alchemy was not a popular sect. Colonnader cosmology was the one most universally respected in man-inhabited space; the most scientific, the most proven. And while it had its variants and deviations, alchemy was not one of them. Alchemists were famous for spreading noxious and dangerous gases, dusts and radiations through their ill-considered experiments, and were forbidden to practice their art on more worlds than not; hence this station on a dead world where they could harm no one but themselves. In place of the stoical calm of the colonnaders, they had a reputation for mental aberration and reckless improvisation, for being unable to restrain their burning zeal for chemical discovery.

By now sufficiently schooled in philosophy to be able to call himself a colonnader, Boaz felt curious about doctrines that were rivals of his own. Alchemical work was exotic enough for him to feel attracted to the alchemists despite their dour and over-intense manner. He became friendly with Dorsuse, the chief artifex at the station, and this individual indulged him to the extent of using him as an untrained assistant in the main laboratory.

The alchemists were indeed contemptuous of danger. Their skin was discolored and bore the marks and scars of many strange burns and lacerations. Boaz alone took the precaution of wearing a face mask in the mercury-laden, vapor-drenched air of the laboratory, and many were those present whose breath came in gasps or whose limbs shook from the intake of similar unholy mixtures over the years.

Boaz counted himself lucky. Since coming to the planet the team of adepts had been preparing a singularly arcane experiment, and it was about to come to culmination. Dorsuse had promised to take him to the firepit to witness the climax.

The object of the operation was to isolate a particularly potent and rarefied form of fire as the alchemists understood the element. They called it *etherial fire*. According to them, its existence was so far hypothetical only. The firepit, dug by the alchemists themselves, was lined with mica and diamond laminate. For nearly a standard year they had been slowly dripping into it a mixture made up of more than forty substances, including plutonium, electronium (a form of matter whose nuclear protons had been replaced by positrons; the substance was electrically neutral but incredibly light, and capable of numerous fanciful molecular configurations impossible for normal matter), mercury which had been treated by a secret process known only to alchemists, and other substances which they also claimed were not known by orthodox science.

The real secret, Dorsuse assured him, lay in the measured proportions by which the ingredients were slowly introduced to one another. A century of experimentation, he told Boaz, had gone into the formula that was now being tried. It was calculated that on the 29th of month three, the meld would be complete, all the ingredients being exactly tempered and suffused. The result should be etherial fire.

Boaz was excited. With Dorsuse and two other alchemists, he stood on the overhanging observation platform on the lip of the pit. Down below was a faint orange-green radiance from a cloudlike mass.

He was wearing dark goggles Dorsuse had given him. The alchemists had goggles, too, but careless as ever, they left them dangling around their necks. On an impulse Boaz tore off his goggles too, and gloried in the stinging sensation in his eyes as the glow fell on them.

He wanted to make the most of this. He switched on rheobase setting three, felicity setting two (he didn't want to lose control by setting too high). Preservation, of course, was already on. He never switched it off.

Glow, glow, orange and green. The now-familiar intensification of vision due to lowered rheobase hit him (lowering the rheobase threshold intensified sensation; raising rheobase dimmed it). The depth of the pit, with its dark, round, brooding walls, the nascent life of the cloudy mass, made him heady with anticipation.

"I think the light is increasing," Dorsuse said.

Another of the alchemists nodded. "Do you think we shall be on schedule this time?"

"Schedule" was an obsessive word with Boaz's hosts. Their theory of chemical operations contained a time factor. Ordinary chemical reactions, which took place immediately or in seconds or minutes, were in their parlance "vulgar" or "common." The arcane chemical processes

took place over time spans of days, months, years, even
decades (there was a legend of an alchemical reaction that
took more than six hundred standard years to take place).
The sought-for transformation of substance, however, usually happened suddenly at the end of this time, and was
supposed to be predictable to within seconds, This was
what was implied by "schedule." In fact, an alchemical
operation was likely to involve a whole sequence of color
changes, transitions between solid, liquid, gas and plasma,
or other signs Boaz was not familiar with, all consequent
on the continued application of the enlivening energy
source, and if any single one of them failed to occur on
time the whole procedure was deemed abortive.

For all that, there was a great deal of self-glorification
in the alchemists' own descriptions of their art. Though
they would speak airily of predicting the outcome of
years-long operations to "within seconds," in practice they
could rarely calibrate their schedules to less than a calen-
dar day.

"Yes, it is increasing," Dorsuse said. He leaned out over
the parapet, craning his neck to get a better view.

"Is there any danger?" Boaz asked tentatively. "How
will the ether-fire manifest itself?"

"Well, we can always get out of the way if anything
alarming looks about to happen. . . ."

As he spoke the incandescent mass exploded. It reared
up the well of the pit in a gaseous flash. The platform sup-
ports were burned through in an instant. Down fell the
platform and its occupants. The etherial fire (for that was
what it truly was) boiled over the rim in a foaming, ex-
panding mushroom head of light.

Paradoxically, it was indescribably beautiful: a golden,
radiant, softly roaring incandescence. Boaz knew this because he did not disappear into the depths of the pit as did
the others. They must have been killed in a split second.
He, by contrast, grabbed the lip of the pit as he fell, and
with a strength he should not have possessed he hung on.

The gentle, beautiful light was not all he knew as he
hung there. Etherial fire only *looked* beautiful, with a
beauty that masked its inner horror, its antipathy to all organic life. It was fire upon fire, fire within fire, fire impounded, compounded, almost playful in its ability to

torture without limit, penetrating his body to the core, to the bones in fact, infusing every cell to some degree.

Boaz should have died within two or three seconds. So would he have, had he been engulfed in ordinary fire, for the heat was intense. His flesh would have turned to shreds of carbon and even his bones, those shining silicon bones, would have melted.

But etherial fire was subtle, rarefied, as tenuous as perfume. It burned in a way that ordinary heat did not. The chemical changes attendant upon combustion took place but leisurely in its presence (the observation platform had been charred to disintegration; it should have been vapourized). Boaz, likewise, burned *slowly* with a burning that soaked deep into his body, into his mind, into his feelings.

Yet if that were all he had to suffer, he might have died in not too large a fraction of a minute. But it was not all. He also had a silicon bones.

Nature bestows one merciful beneficence on the living creatures she generates and touches with waking consciousness. She so arranges their nervous systems that there is a limit to the degree of suffering they can endure. When agony or terror reach a certain traumatic point, the organism immunizes itself against further horror by means of daze, unconsciousness or death. Shock is the ultimate guarantee. The heart stops, blood leaves the brain, catatonia develops.

That was the mistake of the bonemakers, who proved themselves less wise than nature.

For the whole ten minutes that Boaz was engulfed in etherial fire, his preservation function kept his ravaged body working after a fashion. It kept the blood pumping, the nerve cells firing. It insisted, with an implacable preprogramed will, that the ascending reticular system which brings alertness to the brain should not close down.

Boaz was conscious the whole time.

Not only that, he was on rheobase setting three. Put simply, lowered rheobase meant hyperaesthesia. Every sensation was felt with an unnatural keenness—every datum of pain had that extra edge. Not only that, he was on felicity setting two. Everything he received with his senses was being shunted to his emotions.

Boaz grabbled in his mind. Instant insanity might have

been a refuge of sorts, but the preservation function was charged with maintaining not only his physical but also his psychological health. Mental coherence was another matter, however. He called on his bones to help him, trying to mouth trigger syllables as though screaming prayers to the gods.

He was too overwhelmed with pain to have any real control over what his mind pronounced. The heat had probably affected the bone functions, too. Because he did not even have the syllable for what followed.

Felicity retuned itself to setting eight—three settings higher than the bonemakers had allowed him to experience.

His burden of physical agony, already inconceivable in terms of what human awareness can be expected to survive, crashed through the remaining gates of his mind to take possession of the entire gamut of his emotions. Pain that had already stripped his consciousness bare, that burned and whipped him, that transcended all thought or explanation, that had become a living entity, a personality that spoke to him, played with him, raped him, punished him with its enfolding caresses, now had access to the "joy function"—a reservoir of positive emotional energy. It instantly turned that energy negative.

Misery would have been too bland a word to describe the rivers of ultimate horror that flooded and ran through Boaz. It is not often that emotional pain can equal physical pain of even a normal kind. Yet he knew grief that arose from and was the equal of his physical torment. There were no hidden parts to Joachim now. Not a thought, not a feeling, not a memory was not dredged up and drenched permanently in that grief. He howled his suffering until that howl echoed in an emptiness which was his own self, and that self contracted around and became only one thing. PAIN, AGONY, SUFFERING, GRIEF, *repeated and repeated and repeated, forever and ever. Amen.*

The alchemists in the distance heard his screams. They listened to them with curiosity and fascination. How could screams be so seemingly endless in content? How could they seem so much like a new language, for a new world? When the etherial fire at length dissipated (rising through the atmosphere and into space, they said, seeking its proper abode among the stars) they ventured cautiously closer. They found the blackened form of Boaz still clinging as if in rigor mortis to the laminated diamond-and-mica lip of the pit. He wasn't screaming now; the preservation function had robbed him of the physical strength to do so as it commandeered every erg of energy in its desperate fight to keep him alive. They presumed he was dead, of course. They scooped up his charred body and placed it on a wooden board. Then, amazed to find he was still breathing, they carried him into their small surgery, but appeared to think the case hopeless and did nothing for him.

As chance would have it the company ship put down to pick him up only an hour later. The ship's robot doctor, observing that he did not immediately die, consulted Boaz's medical record. Then it did its duty and informed the captain of *his* duty. Boaz was delivered, still suffering, to the bonemakers twenty light-years away.

The bonemakers, in turn, did their duty as they saw it. They set about to repair Boaz. The task was more massive than any they had yet envisioned; it made the mere making of silicon bones seem easy.

And indeed, bones were of no use in a case like this. Every cell, every nerve, every gland, every single metabolic process would have to be closely and permanently regulated by artificial means; truly speaking, Boaz's entire somatic integrity was gone, and would never in future be able to stave off total collapse. On the other hand, all the adp that would be needed could never be packed inside Boaz's frame, not even using bones—and even if some means of incorporating could be found, the bonemakers would have decided firmly against it. So fine were the attunements that were required that bringing the processors into physical contiguity with the ruined *soma* would in short order have led to functional coalescence. Boaz would no longer have been human.

So regulators and *soma* had to be separate, and to house everything necessary to keep his destroyed body miraculously walking, digesting, feeling and thinking would take a building the size of a small dwelling.

But that would effectively have imprisoned him within a

radius of a few miles. The bonemakers chose another course. They felt they owed it to Boaz to do more than merely heal him. They owed him something in recompense.

Knowing of his ambitions, they bought him a ship. A newly built cargo ship, crew-robotized (independent shipkeepers disliked hiring employees), with range enough to allow him to roam almost anywhere, provided he could find cargoes to pay his way. And into that ship they put all the processing. Into it they put the transceivers that linked him to this secret brain, larger than any natural brain since it undertook to keep biological functions running that should have been able to run themselves. The ship was, in fact, a preservation function, but one far more capacious and more penetrating than that put earlier into his silicon bones. Correspondingly, it gave him a survivability that was unparalleled.

The bonemakers' unheated apologies still rang in Boaz's ears. They admitted to having made a serious mistake. It might comfort him to know that other bonemen would benefit from his experience. Future models would have an automatic cutoff on the preservation function to render the owner unconscious beyond a set level of pain, or even to permit him to die. And they were calling in all bones installed so far for modification.

While Boaz and the bonemakers could never be quits, they had done all they could for him. In their opinion he was still far better off than when they had first picked him up off that Corsair spaceground.

His bones, they informed him, were still operable. It made no difference to Boaz. He had never used them since.

Captain Boaz groaned out loud.

AGONY—AGONY—AGONY—

Normal physical pain, however bad, is mentally unrecoverable once it is over. That it happened can be recollected, the nervous system can be permanently depressed by it, but the memory carries no storage facility whereby the experience of it can be relived.

Emotional pain, however, the mind *can* remember, and relive. Boaz's pain had not been normal. It had been physical and emotional all at once, supernal physical pain married to emotional pain of like intensity. And the memory of it bubbled up unbidden, again and again.

And yet such memory was not the worst of it; burdensome though it was, it was but a pale copy of the original. Worse was *knowledge*. The knowledge that it had happened.

In the doctrine of an extinct religion the wicked were consigned after death to a lake of supernatural fire. This fire burned a thousand times more intensely than ordinary fire, and was a thousand times more agonizing. Yet it burned without consuming, and those cast into it burned forever.

Boaz understood the description. He had been dipped into the lake of hellfire.

As if in dim after-image to the brilliant pain-flash, he remembered when, after a long time spent in the medibath, his tissues were mended and he emerged as a lumpy, scarred version of his former self—but only physically. Psychologically he was broken.

Then began the visits of Madrigo, his mentor. Methodically, with sure touches, he began the job of reconstituting Boaz's shattered mentality. Boaz could hear now the mentor's quiet, sympathetic voice. Ataraxy was all. A contented life was impossible without it. Everything that happened, no matter how good or how bad, must simply be accepted, with equanimity.

Madrigo agreed that some experiences were dread enough to overcome even the most highly controlled human consciousness, and Boaz had been through something that could destroy any normal psyche utterly. Without philosophy there would be no hope for him. But there *was* philosophy, and the mind, in the last analysis, was stronger than all, simply because it was eternal while experiences were only temporary.

Ataraxy must be striven for. Pleasure and pain, however intense the degree, must never be acknowledged as a master.

"After all, are not your chosen names *Joachim* and *Boaz*, the two pillars of universal stability?"

"Yes," said Boaz, "but I am beginning to curse those names. . . ."

"Take the large view," the mentor told him. "When the world ends, when all is absorbed in mind-fire, your accident will take on a different aspect. It will not seem fearsome, then."

"No!" Boaz protested with a passion that broke through the resolve that Madrigo had patiently been building in him. "I do not believe mind-fire sees experience as illusory or unreal—that would be to render the creation meaningless! The world is real, mentor, you have taught me that. My sufferings were real! They cannot be mitigated by a change of view!"

To that, Madrigo remained silent.

Boaz slumped in his chair, head and shoulders slouched forward as though he were about to fall out of it. The memories faded, then disintegrated and flew apart like a flock of birds startled by a gunshot.

A set of luminous dials on the wall of the cabin quivered, From the drive down below a fuzzy whine, his constant companion, permeated the cabin.

A chime gonged. It was time to change the fuel rods.

With an effort he lurched reluctantly up from his chair. He flexed his stiffened limbs, and turned up the cabin's dim lighting.

He scanned the dials. He would soon be in Harkio.

Then he would know whether the lead he had was worth anything or not.

Chapter

THREE

BY THIS EDICT:

Experimentation aimed at the establishment of travel through time is forbidden UNDER PAIN OF DEATH.

Experimentation aimed at control over the time flow is forbidden UNDER PAIN OF DEATH.

Experimentation aimed at retrieving objects from past or future states is forbidden UNDER PAIN OF DEATH.

Experimentation aimed at gaining direct consciousness of or retrieving information from past or future states is forbidden UNDER PAIN OF DEATH.

Possession of any artifact or natural object exhibiting one or more of the above properties is forbidden UNDER PAIN OF DEATH. Possession of any document containing explicit data relating thereto is forbidden UNDER PAIN OF DEATH.

Acts of experimentation, research of inquiry into the nature of time are forbidden UNDER PAIN OF LIFE IMPRISONMENT OR DEATH unless with the express permission of the Office of Scientific Regulation. Publication of confirmed or theoretical data relating thereto is forbidden UNDER PAIN OF LIFE IMPRISONMENT OR DEATH unless with the express permission of the Office of Scientific Regulation.

(Bearing the seal of the
Department of Law Propagation.)

Gare Romrey left Karti's in a hurry, leaving his friends there feeling decidedly less friendly. Outplanet in a rented Stardiver, he paused within call range just before going into hype, and dialed through. Being what he was, he was quite unable to resist this last look back.

Karti's Dive Infee Club came up on the cage plate, sour light from the ceiling strips falling on stained walls and tattered furniture. The bar was sticky with spilled drinks to which adhered ash from waft sticks. Only about half a dozen people were visible—the others had decamped in an effort to stop Romrey from reaching the ship ground. They crowded the screen when they realized who was bleeping them.

Up front was the thin-faced redheaded kosher pimp with the archaic cognomen of Jericho Junkie. Romrey flashed him a quick smile.

"I thought I'd just explain, boys—"

"He's offplanet," someone behind Jericho muttered. The purveyor ponce (he supplied a specialized sexual taste involving a rare genetic type of woman, a certain drug and a specially treated aphrodisiac food) glared at Romrey with hot eyes. "*One* chance, Romrey. You've got *one chance* to get back here with the cube. Otherwise—"

"This, you mean?" Romrey held up the half-inch-sized memory cube which Jericho had been selling by lottery and which he had filched just before the numbers were about to be called. "You've got to trust me, boys. I thought of a better plan, that's all. I asked myself what would happen if one of you won the cube. What would you do with it? Go out there and try to land on Meirjain?" He shook his head. "It would be a fiasco. *Me*, now—I can handle a job like that. When I get back I'll split the incomings with you."

Snorts of indignation expressed a general disbelief in his last pronouncement. "Whoever won the cube could have sold it," Jericho said.

Romrey shook his head again. "Negative thinking. This way I—we—strike big."

A bull-shouldered alec shoved Jericho aside and thrust his jaw out at Romrey, who recognized him as Ossuco, a carcass dealer. "We know where you're going, you rat, and we'll catch up with you. I got a feeling *I* would have drawn that ticket. I'd like to know what makes *you* think you could get away with it."

Romrey picked up the pack of cards lying on the control board and fanned them open, holding them up before the cage screen. "*These* told me to do it."

He let them gawp for a moment at the numbered picture cards, before he cut them off.

Then he swiveled his seat to face the engine controls. He gripped the manual handles and pushed them forward. Energy spurted from the fuel rods as the *Stardiver* put on speed. With a shudder he hit c; then he was riding smoothly, heading for the center of the Harkio region where it nearly touched the Brilliancy Cluster.

He was grinning with pleasure when he switched to auto. He always enjoyed going through c on manual.

The journey to Sarsuce would take a few days. He picked up the memory cube again and plugged it into the *'diver*'s starmap. The Brilliancy Cluster came up on the navigation screen. The view was from Sarsuce, or rather from Sarsuce's sun, the Econosphere planet nearest to the cluster. A red arrow blinked on and off, pointing out the spot where Meirjain was due to make its appearance. At the bottom of the screen ran boxed lines of figures, including a date.

Absentmindedly Romrey reached into the larder chute and took out a pinana. He peeled off the orange-hued skin while he studied the screen. It was his favorite fruit: a banana into which the flavor of pineapple had been delicately, genetically blended.

The cluster was, to be sure, a beautiful if familiar sight. Romrey's attention focused on the red arrow, surrounded as it was by piles of vari-colored stars. He read the data box, making a rough estimate of times and distances.

How many other people had this data? It was supposed to be rare, but—

Jericho Junkie claimed to have got it during a trip to

Sarsuce, from the Meirjain tracker himself. Romrey turned from the screen. One hand picked up the deck of cards again, and expertly laid out a row while he bit into the pinana. He frowned as he tried to interpret the sequence. The Inverted Man reversed, followed by the ten of laser rods, followed by the eight of ciboria. . . . He stopped, puzzled. Deceit, leading to fulfilment.

Reading the future was not his forté. Reading a course of action, though, was easier—and in that regard what he had told Jericho was true. The cards *had* instructed him to rob the lottery, although the idea, of course, had been in his mind already.

Romrey, in recent years, had hit upon a practice which relieved life of much of its anxiety. Whenever he came to a point of uncertainty, he consulted the cards, and he did whatever he believed they were telling him to do. If the issue could be reduced to a simple *yes* or *no*, of course, then so much the better.

There was a heady, almost delirious pleasure in not being responsible for his own decisions anymore.

He thought of the poor cruds in Karti's. Planet-huggers for the most part, scarcely been off Kleggisae. A ponce, a carcass dealer, assorted alecs who had found ways of living off the Econosphere Welfare Bureau. Not a prospector among them.

Strictly speaking Romrey wasn't a prospector either. He called himself "a trader with wide interests." But the thought of landing on Meirjain the Wanderer didn't frighten him, and neither did the competition. Neither did he necessarily think of himself as a liar. Would he be generous to his erstwhile friends and colleagues in the Karti Dive Infee, as he had promised, if he made out on Meirjain? Maybe he would, maybe he wouldn't.

He would let the cards decide.

And if they decided against, Ossuco could look for him in every sextile of the Econosphere for all he cared.

Thoughtfully, self-indulgently, he munched the pinana.

In half a standard day Captain Joachim Boaz's business in Harkio was completed. He delivered his cargo, collected the small tail fee, and took off again for Sarsuce, the natural jumping-off point for the Brilliancy Cluster.

Through a hazy atmosphere and what seemed an untypical drove of traffic, he descended onto the ship ground at Wildhart, Sarsuce's largest city—though not the capital, since Sarsuce had none. It was the kind of town he seemed to have spent half his life in, with an atmosphere that did not give him the feeling of being in an authentic place at all, but more like a transit district, a place at the junction of other places, a boom town that had somehow outlived its usefulness so that even to claim a name for itself smacked of fraud. The deception was never more transparent than now. The ship ground was uncommonly full, and Boaz was hard put to squeeze a place for his ship in it. The port proctor's clerk took his fee with an unfriendly brusqueness, as though Boaz were forcing him to connive in something immoral. And when he walked into Wildhart itself the excitement was palpable.

Boaz scowled. All these strangers. He did not like to be one of a crowd, and it was certain they were mostly after the same thing he was—though for different reasons.

The sun slanted from the west. But overhead there hung what appeared to be a giant bauble in the sky, like a lantern hung from a festival tree; a hundred times larger than the sun itself, and glowing palely with a multihued mass of point sources, even in broad daylight. That was the Brilliancy Cluster, with its estimated eight thousand close-packed stars, the place where *pure* prospectors went. It had no settled planets, no properly mapped interior—in fact not a lot of planets at all, since nearly all its stars had quirkishly opted to form planetless double, triple and quadruple sun systems.

But it did have one very famous planet, a planet of fable that until now had been seen only once: Meirjain the Wanderer, a planet which had no sun of its own but which instead swung from star to star like an interstellar comet, weaving an apparently random path within the cluster.

On average the stars of Brilliancy were only light-hours apart, allowing Meirjain to steer a miraculous, sinuous course which gave it an equable climate for nearly all the time. This remarkable feat was taken as evidence that the Wanderer's motion was the result of artifice, though not everyone thought so—the astronomer Ashojin had calculated that Meirjain followed a thermal isocline due to the competing geodesics of surrounding stars. In fact very little could be stated of the Wanderer with certainty. It had been discovered three centuries ago. Men had landed on it, had sampled its treasures. Then, through the carelessness or ignorance of its discoverers, it had been allowed to disappear again, melting untrackably into the Brilliancy Cluster like a molecule of sugar in colored water.

And now, three centuries later, word had it that the Wanderer had been sighted again; its course tracked to the point where it would emerge on the edge of the Cluster in the gravisphere of a particular star. Which star, and when, was what all these people were here to find out.

Boaz pushed his way through a jostling crowd of naked nymphgirls, purveyors, vendors, steer narks and modsuited shipkeepers—some of them cargo carriers like himself, perhaps, but more likely prospectors. He ignored the overhead adholo flashes which tried to beam enticing images into the retinas of his eyes. He moved down the avenue—it seemed that every town he stopped in had an avenue just like this one, as though there were only one town in the whole galaxy, capable of manifesting itself everywhere—until he came to the arcaded entrance of a rest room.

He turned into it. The room was large and dome-shaped. It was as if he were back in Hondora, except that this place was busier. He found an empty table and sat down, signing a robot to bring him a drink while he surveyed the people around him.

Information was being offered here, his ship told him. Sipping the milky cocoin the robot delivered, he became aware of someone at his elbow. A small man, his body swathed in buff and orange bands, slipped into the chair opposite. Boaz disliked him immediately. His smile was too ingratiating.

"Good day, shipkeeper!" the stranger said jovially. "Looking to land on Meirjain?"

"What is it to you?" Boaz became aware that the man had followed him from the ship ground.

"Most people who come in are looking for it. You know what the hottest property around here is, I suppose?"

"No."

"The hottest property is numbers. Coordinate numbers. That tell you where and when Meirjain will appear."

The swathed man turned to indicate a table in the center of the room where a dumpy, togaed individual sat talking desultorily with two others and toying with a set of gambling cubes. His eyes were downcast. Boaz recognized him as a person who spent most of his time *waiting*. Waiting for the right customer to come along.

"See that alec over there? He has the numbers. He's one of about ten people on Sarsuce who have them. But it's information that costs a *lot*."

"Why should it? Meirjain will become visible soon."

"Not soon enough. Haven't you heard?" The other raised his eyebrows. "The Wanderer's been put off-limits. An econosphere cruiser is on its way. Nobody is going to get down on Meirjain that isn't able to jump the gun and get to the coordinate point ahead of that cruiser. So you see, it's the coordinates or nothing."

"This is a wild story. I don't believe you."

The man sighed. "How blunt. It's almost quaint, really. You needn't believe *me*." He reached into a swathe and placed a news card on the table, tracing his finger round the dial. "See for yourself."

Boaz picked up the thin wafer. The holoflash hit his retinas. In urgent, colored script, he read: ALL CITIZENS ARE ADVISED AND WARNED THAT THE PLANET KNOWN AS "MEIRJAIN THE WANDERER" AND ASSOCIATED WITHIN THE LIMIT OF THE BRILLIANCY CLUSTER IS BY ORDER OF THE DEPARTMENT OF LOCATIONAL AFFAIRS PLACED UNDER ABSOLUTE PROHIBITION. NO LANDING IS TO BE MADE ON SAID PLANET NOR ANY SCAN CARRIED OUT EXCEPT BY OFFICIAL ORDER. PENALTIES WILL BE POSTED IN THE AMOUNT OF TWENTY YEARS LABOR OR FIVE HUNDRED THOUSAND PSALTERS. . . .

Thoughtfully he laid down the card. The penalties were largely bluff. The econosphere, as the great rambling empire of man-inhabited space called itself, was in a state of semi-disintegration; spasmodically tyrannous, but just as often unable to impose any effective government whatsoever over innumerable worlds. The government would depend on the arriving cruiser to enforce the edict. . . .

"If you still don't believe me," his informant said softly, "there's a public announcement on every two-hour."

"In these circumstances," Boaz pointed out, "*no* one is going to land on Meirjain."

"Some people reckon they can. Econosphere law doesn't count for a lot in this neck of the woods; that cruiser has a long way to come. Word has it that those who know in advance where the Wanderer is due will beat the law to the drop."

Boaz's mind turned to what might be behind the ban, which bore all the hallmarks of official panic. There was uncounted wealth on Meirjain; its dead civilization was a treasure house. But most valuable of all, of course, were what Boaz was after—time-jewels, gems able to refract light through time as well as space. It was the only known example of time modification by physical—and probably artificial—means.

Something about these gems frightened the econosphere government, Boaz reasoned. He had tried to track down some of the jewels that had been taken from the Wanderer on the first landing three centuries ago. To all intents and purposes they had vanished from existence, hidden away, secreted—perhaps even destroyed, he suspected—by government agencies.

His conclusion gave him hope. If the authorities feared the gems, then they had a use. . . .

"The alec's name is Hansard," Boaz's informant was saying. "Do you want me to talk to him?"

"I don't have money in the amount he would probably ask."

"You have a ship. A fine ship."

Boaz grunted. "Without a ship, what good are coordinates?"

"Leave it to me."

While Boaz watched, the swathed man walked to Hansard and leaned over to talk to him. Hansard glanced at Boaz, a perfunctory, predatory glance. He nodded, as his eyes returned to the table.

The swathed man beckoned. The others left the table as Boaz stepped over and took the seat that was offered. Hansard's gaze flicked up to him and back to his cubes again. He was smiling to himself.

"A fine ship you have, I'm told. What's its name?"

"It's my ship; it doesn't need a name."

"Well, never mind. . . ."

Hansard scattered the play blocks and reached in his pocket. He pulled out a memory cube and held it up. "I had four of these. I've got two left. I paid good money for them and I'd like to make a profit, but I'm not adamant about it. I place it in the lap of the gods."

"That's normal commercial practice."

"Correct. I'm a gambler. Double or quits. One throw. If you win, you have the numbers and you still have your ship so you can use them. If I win, I take your ship. You won't have any use for the numbers then, anyway."

"I guess not," Boaz said. The idea that he would gamble with his ship as a stake caused him a wry amusement. He had known this was all wrong from the outset, and now the beam that stretched out to him from the ship ground confirmed it.

He cheats; the blocks are loaded, his ship whispered to him. And then: *Also, his merchandise is worthless.*

As a thief, Hansard was stupid. He piled cons on top of one another, multiplying the risk to himself.

"You're overdoing it," Boaz said aloud. "A good swindle doesn't need redundancy."

He rose and strode away. Back in the avenue the public announcement was beginning. CITIZENS ARE ADVISED AND WARNED. . . . Passersby paused, glanced up to let the flashing letters strike their eyes the better, then walked on unconcerned.

Boaz had the picture now. Wildhart would be crawling with dealers offering fake coordinates. And the real coordinates? How many people had those? Half a dozen? Two or three? Or only one?

He felt little doubt that the story of the race with the government cruiser was true. Otherwise there would be little demand for coordinates at all.

It was beginning to look like a problem.

Romrey had forgotten how kinky the fringe planets were. In former empires depravity had festered first in the central urban areas. In the econosphere, it seemed instead to arise in the nearly lawless peripheral provinces, working its way inward to eat steadily away at the fabric of morality.

The girl had picked him up at an eatery on the night of his arrival. The eatery served spicecrab, a dish banned on many conservative worlds whose flesh contained compounds related to L-dopamine and alpha androstinol. Romrey had damned the expense. In his euphoria at arriving on Sarsuce he had wanted to try something new.

But what the girl, whose name was Mace, hungered for was *too* new as far as he was concerned. The alpha androstinol had done its stuff (that was why she had gone there: to find a man whose pheromones excited her). But later, when they rented a play room not even the L-dopa could carry him through the scene she wanted. She wanted him to kill her.

Romrey had never done that before. The idea repelled him. And he told her so. Perversely (maybe it was the spicecrab again) his refusal excited her even more.

Since then, she had been pursuing him. In eateries, in drinking houses, in the street, hanging around outside the door of his lodging, she would sidle up to him. *"Kill me."* she would whisper in his ear. It was a determined kind of seduction he found horrifying. As if he were the one who was to be defiled.

In one way, he supposed, he could see some sense in it. On the night of their first meeting Mace had told him she was a bonewoman. Bone people were usually colonnaders, and colonnaders believed that consciousness—mind-fire, as they called it—was not limited by space or time. She probably had no real conception of personal extinction; she thought her same consciousness would awaken in the clone body she had somewhere.

A colonnader had once explained it to him in terms of the death and rebirth of the universe. "We never die, really," he had said. "When we are resurrected in the next turn of the wheel, it's our own same consciousness that lives again."

Romrey was skeptical. He wondered, though, whether Mace's clone also had silicon bones. That would mean she had a lot of money. . . .

He had resolved to ignore her until she eventually wearied of the game, but he had not reckoned on a deadly trick she had up her sleeve. He awoke one night and became aware that someone was in his room, moving clumsily.

He waved his hand at the service panel, flooding the room with light. Mace was there, naked, her voluptuous breasts flopping (she did not follow the breastless nymphgirl fashion). As the light came on, her hand went to her hair and pulled out what appeared to be a strand. The strand stiffened and went silvery. It was a paraknife.

In almost the same instant she flung herself toward the bed. Romrey rolled aside. The knife stabbed down where he had been and sliced his shoulder. He hardly felt it at first. Then the stinging pain and the sight of his dripping blood brought his senses to a furious awakening.

"You bitch!"

They stood facing one another over the bed. She still pointed the paraknife at him, her shoulders hunched. Her face was slack. Her lips drooped, in a way that made him imagine something lascivious was dripping from them.

Then she began to giggle. "I'm going to have you," she told him. "You'll have to kill me, because if you don't *I'm going to kill you!* It's you or me—get it?"

Gasping with passion and fright, she lunged at him again. He retreated, but she clambered over the bed to get at him. "You'd better do it," she breathed. "You'd better do it now. Or I'll get you sooner or later. Creep up on you—stick it in—bet you got no other body to wake up in. Right?"

"Right," he said harshly. He caught her wrist in his hand, holding the knife away from him, while she kicked desperately at his crotch with vermilion-painted toes. A rage was boiling up in him to think how close to death he might have been, accompanied by a feeling of heat and a pounding in his ears—an unfamiliar reaction he would not have guessed he could make.

"All right." His words came thickly. "If that's how you want it—"

He twisted her hand, forcing her to drop the knife. He punched her in the stomach. She folded up on the bed. He fell on her. A mist was before his eyes as he felt his hands go round her throat.

Passing on the avenue a few yards distant, Captain
Joachim Boaz paused.

The ship's beams were sweeping the district, searching
for information. What they brought him in this instance
was far from what he sought, but it caught his attention
just the same.

The scene was the distasteful kind he had glanced at on
many occasions and then turned away from. He would
have done so now except for one extra piece of information. The beam told him: *She has no replacement body*.
Then: *He believes she has*.

Boaz hesitated, of a mind to keep to his own business
and pass on, but his colonnader training told on him. He
turned into an alley that ran through a small maze of
rented rooming shacks. His ship told him when he had
come to the right place; told him what was happening behind the lithoplast wall. The entrance was on the other
side of the building, and he judged there was no time to
go looking for it.

He called on the ship to flood his tissues with toughness
and strength. He attacked the thin wall with the edge of
his hand, chopping right through it in three sharp blows.
Then dust and frayed fragments were raining down about
him as, like some kind of demolition engine, he burst
through the partition and confronted the startled pair.

Romrey rose slowly from the bed. To him, Boaz must
have been a frightening sight, and he began to edge
toward the cupboard where he kept his gun.

Boaz raised a monitory hand.

"You should be warned that you are laying yourself
open to a charge of murder," he rumbled.

Romrey huffed, momentarily overcoming his surprise.
"What are you talking about? It's legal here."

"Only when the terminated party has a working linked-
up clone."

"What?" Romrey murmured. His eyes sought Mace's.
"But don't you have . . . ?"

Mace was rubbing her neck. She winced. Then she
shrugged.

"So I'm tired of life. So what?"

"And what about *me?*" Romrey's anger returned. He

bent over her, his fist raised in her face. "I would have gone to the chamber for you!"

"Be gallant. Say I'm worth it."

Mace slipped from under him and stepped to where she had dropped some clothes near the door. Deftly she slipped into a shiftlike robe, smoothing it down. She pulled up her hair and tied it in a snood.

Boaz stared at her. Through her ostentatious unconcern, certain facts were visible. First, very fine white lines in the skin, unnoticeable by most but discernible to Boaz, told him she had silicon bones. But that did not mean she was a colonnader—though still rare, bones were being acquired by more and more people these days, not all of them colonnaders.

Boaz did not think she was a colonnader. The stoical quality of ataraxy was not in her face. In his judgment she was pure epicurean, and lived for the senses.

And, yes, she was tired of life. She had chosen an exotic style of suicide without a thought for the consequences for her victim—something a colonnader would never do.

While she dressed momentary looks of concentration came to her face, suggesting to Boaz that she was switching off her bone functions one by one, detumescing from a plateau that had never been reached. Was she relieved—or just disappointed? He tore his gaze away as the man spoke.

"Are you law enforcement?"

Boaz smiled faintly. "Not the law you are talking about. No, I am nothing official."

The man was peering through the hole Boaz had made in the wall, as if expecting to see something there. "What other kind of law is there?"

"He's talking about cosmic ethical law," the woman said acidly. "He's just a goddammed busybody. A fully boned, paid-up, stuck-up ethical pain in the neck." Boaz realized she took his supernormal strength for evidence that he, too, wore silicon bones in his body, and she had put two and two together.

"I'm surprised you ever got replaced, with your attitude," he told her. "Replaced" was how bone people referred to their transformation.

"The surgeon wasn't a colonnader either. See, busy-body? The ethic is disintegrating."

"Perhaps that is why you wish to end your life? Those who devised silicon bones intended them for people with philosophical training."

"Maybe." The tiredness in the girl's eyes struck Boaz. The man, meanwhile, looked from her to Boaz in bewilderment.

"Look here," he said to Boaz, "thanks for saving my neck, but why don't you two lunatics just clear off and let me get some sleep?"

"As you wish," Boaz said. He made for the door, but then the ever-present ship beam, emanating from a processing load that all this time had been sifting and guessing with the data it was collecting from the scene, made a suggestion.

Both of them could be useful to you.

He turned. "Could it be you are here on Sarsuce waiting for the Wanderer?"

Romrey made a wry face. "Sure. And I've got coordinates, too."

"False ones?"

"Probably. But how would I know? I bought them back in Iridan."

"They are fake. It is almost certain." Boaz turned to Mace. "And you?"

She tossed her head. "Why would someone with a yen for extinction be searching for anything—except death?"

Boaz waited. She relented. "All right. Not me, I don't give a damn for anything. I belong to a man called Radalce Obsoc. One more collector's item. He wants to get down to Meirjain. He wants it bad."

Boaz picked out only what was relevant from her cryptic comments. "You belong to him. Is that why you want to die?"

"Maybe. I've been with him a long time. I just felt tired."

"Your will to live has been drained away through indulgence in the senses."

"Maybe. But then I'm into pleasure, not power like you."

It was understandable that she should misjudge him. Boaz surveyed them both. They were an unlikely pair.

"There might be some benefit in our working together."

Romrey had worked his way through bewilderment and incredulity. Now he was merely puzzled. "How?"

"You are aware that it is going to be very difficult to land on Meirjain without knowing the position of its appearance beforehand. We can take it that all those coordinates offered here in Wildhart and elsewhere are false, and indeed in such circumstances it would be impossible to identify the real ones among the fake. Special talents are needed to track down who has the real ones. A detective could do it, perhaps. . . ."

"Obsoc already hired a detective," Mace said. "He got nowhere."

"So what are these special talents, and why do we have them?" Romrey asked acidly.

Boaz stood motionless. He had no answer.

"You can read the future, maybe?" Romrey persisted.

Seriously, Boaz shook his head. "By no means."

"*I* can read the future," Romrey said

Boaz watched carefully as he reached into a drawer in the bedside table. "I read the future with these," he said. "And I'm going to read it now."

He had taken out a deck of cards and proceeded to lay out ten of them on the table, after a quick shuffle. "The issue is a simple one. Do I throw in with you, or do I not?" Romrey's lean face was intent as he laid down the cards. "A positive answer is a score that's above average. Negative, below average."

Briefly he reckoned up. "Well, that's fairly positive. A hundred and one. It looks like we're partners, whoever you are. And who the hell are you, anyway?"

"I am Captain Joachim Boaz."

"Shipkeeper?"

"Yes." Boaz was gazing at the cards with interest. As Romrey swept them up and laid them down, he stepped over to examine them, glancing at Romrey for permission.

"They're colonnader cards," Romrey told him.

Boaz thumbed through them. "Not colonnader," he stated. "This is a perverted set, muddied with occultism."

There were in fact many variants on the original colonnade pack (itself reconstructed from a pre-scientific pack
of great antiquity), most of them produced by deviant
philosophical or arcane sects. This one was typical. Artisti-
cally it was very accomplished, but the images were altered and adorned with additional symbolism which was
often incorrect and also tended to obliterate much of the
carefully inculcated subtlety of the original. The Priestess,
for instance, a simple but enormously potent figure in the
true colonnade version, was here cluttered with a number
of extraneous signs—in her hair, in her right hand, under
her left foot. These symbols were drawn from the aberrant
occultism of the sect that had construed them, and in that
sense had meaning. But to a colonnader they were simply
irrelevant.

"So you base your decisions on simple chance?" he said
to Romrey. "Play cubes would be sufficient for that."

"Not on chance, no." Romrey shook his head. "That's
no ordinary deck of cards. Look closely at the material.
The cards have adp in them."

"All such cards do—these, for instance." With a slow
movement Boaz brought out his own deck. "To make the
pictures move."

"No, no, these have much more. They are *all* adp."

The cards had a micalike finish. They were, as Romrey
had said, made of adp substance, much like silicon bones.
"These are magical cards," Romrey said. "Mystic cards.
They respond to events going on around them. They are
never wrong. In fact, they can *create* events too."

"Yes, if you are improvident enough to let them guide
all your actions," Boaz remarked.

He had to admit that the cards had a charm all of their
own. Even the aberrant symbolism added up to a certain
bizarre profundity. And he reminded himself that some of
the deviant sects, as they passed down the hidden lanes
and by-ways of thought, often made surprising discoveries.

Just the same, his background made him skeptical of
Romrey's claims, so much so that his lip curled.

However, his ship had presumably, during its surveillance of the city over the past few days, seen this man
using the cards for divination—something which true

colonnaders looked upon as pure superstition. If his ship took it seriously, then so did Boaz.

Romrey began pulling on some garments. Boaz turned to the woman. "And what can your man Obsoc contribute?"

"Him?" She rolled her eyes to the ceiling. "Money. He's rich. He's got his own big yacht orbiting up there, and it's armed, pretty heavily. Probably it could even take on that government cruiser that's coming."

"Can you arrange a meeting with him?"

"If he thinks you can do him any good."

Boaz nodded. Events had changed rapidly for all three of them in the past few minutes, he thought. But people were used to fast transitions, in this modern world.

Radalce Obsoc was a tall, stooped man with bulging eyes. His nose was small and hooked, exactly like an owl's beak, and his thin-lipped mouth was equally small.

His appearance was in curious contrast with the red-haired sensuous-looking Mace Meare, as Boaz had come to know her. Their relationship, however, was not hard to fathom. She was a paid pleasure girl, on permanent contract.

The pleasure, it was understood, was to be hers. Obsoc himself was not a sensuous man: he was a collector, his passions cerebral, who required to have among his possessions a beautiful woman who could plumb the depths of erotic delight. Silicon bones gave Mace that, and Obsoc's enjoyment was the voyeur's one of watching her attain the transports of that delight—with whom, or what, or by herself (Obsoc had a complete collection of sexual appurtenances) did not matter. Boaz doubted if he ever actually touched her himself.

Obsoc collected many things, but his real passion was for jewels. He practically raged at Boaz when he spoke of them. He possessed, he said, specimens of all *but one* of the nine thousand and thirty-four known gem classifications, including the largest natural diamond ever found, weighing over half a ton (this was a mere curiosity, since single-crystal diamonds of up to twenty tons had been synthesized). His cold store contained the complete range of low-temperature gems, including rare varieties of ice of surpassing beauty, produced only under the freak conditions of isolated sunless planets (and far exceeding his half-ton diamond in value). He had an impact technetium sapphire—one of the only two specimens ever found. No price could be put upon his collection; it was unique. He had stipulated that it was to remain intact after his death, and he doubted if any individual would be wealthy enough to buy it. It would, perhaps, become a trust to the glory of the econosphere.

"There is but one gem, sir, that I do not possess," he said in almost ferocious tones to Boaz, "and that is a time-gem from Meirjain the Wanderer. The lack of it makes an intolerable gap in my collection, and I am determined to repair it. Furthermore, the fewer are in circulation the better pleased I shall be. Present circumstances, therefore, meet with my approval to some extent—if all goes well."

"You'd like it better if you could be the only one to land on Meirjain, I suppose?" Romrey interjected.

"You grasp my meaning quite correctly. But you need fear no treachery on my part. I have an unbending sense of probity, and will deal loyally with all members of our little party."

They were in the main cabin of Boaz's ship. He strongly disliked entertaining strangers, or indeed anyone, within this, his private domain (it was like inviting someone into his own body), but the proposed exercise called for it.

He sat next to Romrey at the small circular table. To his left was Mace, and opposite him was Obsoc. Romrey was expertly shuffling his cards. "Are you ready, Captain?"

Curtly Boaz nodded.

"Then we must all concentrate. You especially, Captain. Concentrate on what it is we're looking for."

For Boaz that was easy, despite his feeling slightly ridiculous about the proceedings. He had been obliged to swallow his skepticism in order to make the experiment, which consisted of marrying the cards' reputed function with his ship's special data-gathering ability. Also, he had been obliged to divulge something of that ability. The other three now had some idea—though not a complete one—that it was the ship that kept Boaz alive.

Romrey made a brief salutation, raising his hand perpendicular to his face in a cryptic sign. "To the force that orders events."

Slowly Romrey began to lay down cards, speaking as he did. "This deck was issued by the Carborundum Order, which I don't think exists any more. Anyway I was never a member of it—I'm a straight sort of alec, really. I don't even know what carborundum means."

"It is a carbon compound once used for polishing," Boaz supplied quietly. "The Carborundum Order taught a technique they termed 'polishing the mirror.' The mirror being the mirror of mind."

"Is that so? Well, to get down to it, in the Carborundum deck the four suits stand, among other things, for the four points of the compass on planets that have a magnetic field. So we ought to be able to locate which part of the city to look in."

"If our man is in Wildhart at all," Mace pointed out.

Romrey had dealt five cards. "He is," he said, pointing to the first, which was The Vehicle, showing a gorgeous chariotlike ship surging through space, sometimes dipping into planetary atmospheres, past shining cities or even under oceans.

"This is the perfect card of assent and victory," he said. "It tells us we are right in our assumption. Now, we have two picture cards and three suit cards—two wings, and one cubes. Wings predominate, and stand for north. Therefore he is in the north of the city. But cubes are also present, and they stand for west. So he's in the northwest, or more probably the north-northwest."

He peered thoughtfully at the other picture card, as though hoping for some extra clue in its motions. It was the Inverted Man. "Note that his head enters a deep shaft. It could mean that our target is underground." He darted a look at Boaz. "Can your beams reach down there?"

"It depends how deep," Boaz said. "Shall I begin?"

Romrey hesitated, fingered the next card in the deck, then pushed it back. "Okay."

Boaz slumped, his fist falling to the table with a thump.

He called on his ship, and down below them the innards of one of the big casings geared up, sending beams lunging softly forth. Out, out, up into towers, down into base-

ments, sorting through a collage of Wildhart's innumerable
private scenes.

As on previous occasions, Boaz noted to himself how
repetitious were those scenes. Human life centered around
only a few activities. People ate, drank, slept, quarreled,
fought, made love, gambled, studied, worked. It was like a
number matrix in which nearly all the numbers were the
same. But of course this was Wildhart, a border town. In a
hundred places around the city men and women were sub-
mitting to sex death. There was much robbery, as well as
murder—a crime cheapened today by its erotic associations. As well as debauchery in all its most inventive
forms.

After getting his bearings, Boaz followed Romrey's suggestion and concentrated on the substreet levels, muttering
a monologue to which Romrey listened intently while laying down more cards, trying to interpret them into suggestions as to which direction Boaz should veer in.

Such a rapid, bewildering overseeing of the life of the
city was tiring. And frustrating. After an hour Boaz
stopped, exhausted. They had got nowhere.

"This is no use," he said. "We are making fools of ourselves with those cards."

"I don't reckon so."

"It is ridiculous. I grant they have a lot of adp. So
what? *How can that affect their order when shuffled?*"

Romrey frowned. "I heard something about that once,
but I didn't understand it. These cards are locked into the
structure of the world somehow. They are never wrong,
provided you trust them. But sometimes you have to do a
rerun."

Boaz snorted, glancing scornfully first at Obsoc and
then at Mace. Romrey was shuffling again. "We'll start
from the beginning," he decided stubbornly.

Once more he laid down five cards. The first was the
Vehicle. "Again the Vehicle!" he announced triumphantly.
"Again the Inverted Man! But look here."

The hand was uncannily similar to the first one, so
much so that Boaz suspected sleight of hand. There were
two picture cards and three suit cards. And two of the suit
cards were wings, as before. But the other was laser rods,
not cubes.

"The first reading misled us," Romrey muttered. "Of course—the cubes had a low value, and was not reliable. Here we have the nine of rods, which is more definitive. The coordinates are to be found in the north-northeast, not north-northwest."

Wearily Boaz took up the hunt again. And suddenly he seemed to go in rapport with Romrey. He was telling him where he was and what he saw, and Romrey was slapping down card after card, telling him which way to move and whether he was getting closer or farther.

Romrey himself seemed to go into a daze. He held each hand of five fanned before his face as if playing one of the old games like poker or gin rummy. And he talked, spinning a story out of the cards, sometimes seeming to be ahead of Boaz. Like an invisible spirit, the shipkeeper moved into a semi-derelict area, drifting past broken walls of HCferric that inadequately hid the derelict human beings who sheltered behind them, gliding over dusty unused roadways littered with urban detritus.

Again and again the Inverted Man was turning up, like a flashing locator signal. It told them that Boaz was warm. Then he went through the wall of what appeared to be a deserted warehouse. The ship had found something there, he knew. Moldy abandoned bales of some sort of fiber were stacked to one side. Without pause, the floor rose up to him. He went through it, down into a series of cellars.

One of them had been converted into makeshift living quarters. On a low couch lay a sleeping figure. Beside it, on the floor, was a dish containing a white powder.

Boaz scanned the rest of the room. There was little furniture. The one door bore steel bonds and at the four corners of the room were antennaed boxes. These were guard devices which, to the credit of his ship, the search beams did not appear to have triggered.

This is the man, the ship told him, *who went into the Brilliancy Cluster and detected Meirjain. He has the data.*

"I've found him," Boaz said out loud.

The other three leaned close. "Have you fixed the location?" Obsoc asked.

"I can find it again."

"Who is he?" asked Mace curiously.

"A prospector. He's drugged right now. I think he's an addict. It looks like plutosnow."

"Oh, by the Fire," Mace said, unconscious of using the colonnader oath, "no wonder he didn't make it to Meirjain first time." The effects of plutosnow were erratic. It produced bursts of unusual energy and ability, interspersed with an almost total lack of will. Anything achieved by its use usually had to be finished by somebody else.

"Perhaps the whole story is a fantasy he started," Obsoc suggested worriedly. "Perhaps Meirjain is not due to appear."

"I doubt it," Boaz said. "One side effect of plutosnow is an aversion to untruth. This character may have opened his mouth too much and then holed up for his own protection. Or else he gave the numbers to a few people and then holed up."

"If the econosphere takes it seriously, so can we," Romrey said.

Boaz nodded agreement. He looked at Obsoc. It was now up to the trillionaire to play his part and organize the seizure of the needed information. In the circumstances it scarcely seemed necessary. Boaz felt he could take the cellar on his own.

Obsoc's grasp on realities, however, betokened more than a nodding acquaintance with such operations. "We must move carefully," he said with a grave air. "There are men in Wildhart whose interest in this matter matches our own, and they are totally ruthless. Did you know that the Hat brothers are here? Also Father Larry and his girls. Perhaps you do not know of these people. I assure you they are very resourceful and they will be watching to see if anyone is about to make a move. Yes. . . . Then of course the econosphere undoubtedly has agents here, though whether they command any resources worth speaking of is a different matter." He pondered. "I take it he has defenses?"

"There is a guard system. I didn't see anything else."

"I will hire some people who know how to deal with these things. Meanwhile you'd better give me the exact location."

The collector attended closely while Boaz drew a rough map and described the warehouse. "Good. Well, our work here would seem to be finished. Are you coming: Mace, my dear?"

The girl looked almost appealingly at Boaz. "I'll follow you a little later, Radalce. I'd like to rest here a while longer—if you don't mind, Captain Boaz."

Though he would have preferred her to go, Boaz shrugged his consent. Obsoc looked his craggy body up and down, an obvious thought dawning on him. "Well, enjoy yourself, my dear. I'll send the runabout back for you."

He and Romrey left. When Boaz came back from seeing them down the flowrail she was still sitting at the table. As he came close her hand glided up and gently stroked his leg.

He drew back. "You must not do that, Mace. You cannot expect to entice me into dalliance."

"You're not *that* much of a colonnader!"

"So to speak."

"But you have bones. How can you refuse such pleasure?"

"I never use my bones, Mace. They have been switched off for many years."

"A stoic indeed!"

"Pleasure is a poor thing to me. My life is set in one direction."

"Oh, you're a mystic, bent on self-transcendence," she said, misunderstanding him. "But that puzzles me. Here you are going all out after time-gems. It could only be for the money. Greed for money doesn't square with sensual abstention—does it?"

"It is not for money."

"Then what?" She frowned.

"Never mind." Boaz waved his hand in annoyance.

"You wished to end your life."

"And you interfered. That was very sanctimonious of you."

"It was not because of you. You tried to implicate someone else, in a way that would have had harmful consequences for them. That was unfair."

She looked unabashed. "Do you still intend to end your life?"

She smiled self-consciously, as though wanting to avoid

the subject. "There's no such thing," she said flippantly. "You're a colonnader, you know that. The world returns, and we return with it. There is no death."

"You are not a colonnader."

"I don't have to be. Everybody knows it's true. Science has proved it."

"Yes, that is so." He paused, deliberating, before he spoke again. "But as a consideration, it is too abstract an idea for most people. Even if they take it seriously, the prospect of dreamless sleep for the next nine hundred trillion years is sufficient inducement for the intended suicide. So I ask you again: is it still your intention?"

"I don't know." She dropped her eyes to the table. "When you came bursting in like that, it sort of broke my rhythm."

"Is death really the only thrill left?"

"Well it's one thrill anyway." She glanced up at him again. Her eyes were mischievous. "Want me to tell you what it's like?"

"Not now," Boaz said. "Not now. And leave Romrey alone, as far as that is concerned."

Approaching the warehouse unseen was a problem. Obsoc's hirelings had picked out a route which minimized the open ground to be crossed, and they carried gadgets which were supposed to keep the guard devices silent, but it was still debatable whether the party would enter undetected.

It was night and Sarsuce was moonless, but the placing of the Brilliancy Cluster was such as to send a glow through the whole atmosphere, so that every solid object was surrounded by a haze of shadow. Boaz stirred, crouching behind a low wall, and watched the three raiders as they edged into the light of Brilliancy.

Romrey was crouched stock-still beside him, peering over the wall with the intentness of a stoat. Obsoc was not present; he awaited their report back in his apartment.

The raiders raced suddenly across the stone-strewn ground to fetch up like shadows against the warehouse wall. As they went, something caused Boaz to look to the right of the building. He saw a human figure in a close-fitting catsuit flit away, loping with head down. "Look," he whispered to Romrey. But then it was gone.

A billow of fine dust expanded from the base of the warehouse as the team disintegrated a hole in it. "They're going in," Romrey whispered hoarsely. Boaz could feel his excitement. They watched as two men went inside. The third man paused, waited, then beckoned to Boaz and Romrey. They scrambled over the wall and ran lightly to join the team.

The interior of the warehouse was as Boaz had already seen it. Obsoc's men, wearing light energy armor, moved across the floor, holding out ring antennae parallel to it. They were looking for the trapdoor entrance. One of them, a bland-faced, plump man, abruptly stopped and held up a hand.

"Here it is," he murmured, "but it's too well protected."

"We'll dust in through the floor," one of his companions said, referring to the disintegration process. He pulled out a grenade.

"Wait." The other was listening to his readings through an earphone. A look of surprise crossed his face. "It's already been opened. We can go through."

"He forgot to lock it?"

Already Boaz could guess how events were turning out. But he said nothing while the three cautiously opened the thick hinged plate, alert for traps, and lowered themselves into the cellar below. He followed, and then Romrey. It was as he expected.

The plump man was inspecting a prone body on the matted floor. "He's dead," he announced. "Sonic gun." It was the prospector Boaz had seen asleep on the couch.

"I saw someone run off just as we got here," he informed.

"Damn. Somebody beat us to it."

"Maybe they missed it," Romrey said anxiously. "Look around. Look for a memory cube."

"We'll look. But we won't find it. This was an official killing." Another of the hirelings picked up a card from the floor. It bore a silver eagle—the emblem of the econosphere. "A government agent was here."

"Most likely there never was any external record," the third raider said. "He probably carried the data in his ad-plant."

"Can you be sure that card's genuine?" Boaz asked querulously.

"It's genuine." The hired raider sounded resigned as he examined the document, tilting it in the light to read ingrained patterns. "These are pretty difficult to forge. And eco agents always leave them after an enforcement job."

"It's a way of displaying the long arm of the ecosphere," the other raider said in all seriousness. He flipped open a communicator. "Shall I report to our employer, or will you?"

"I'll do it." He took the communicator and began to press out Obsoc's code.

Romrey was standing over the body of the murdered man, shaking his head. "The government certainly does want to keep Meirjain off limits, to just wipe this poor alec out like this. I wonder what they're afraid of?"

The leader of the hirelings shrugged. "It beats me. The people who got down last time didn't find anything so dangerous, from what I've heard. They all came back in one piece."

Boaz got through to Obsoc. On the matt-like surface of the screen he could see the lounge of his apartment, though Obsoc did not show himself. His dry, petulant voice came through. "Yes? How is it?"

"This is Captain Boaz, Citizen Obsoc," Boaz said politely. "I'm afraid it isn't any use. A government agent got here before us. Almost certainly the data has been wiped out. It probably doesn't exist anywhere now."

"It doesn't matter," Obsoc's voice said. "Not in the least. Something has happened in the last few minutes."

He paused. "There's a blanket broadcast coming out of Brilliancy. It must be from Meirjain. It gives the emergence coordinates. They're common property now."

"But that doesn't make sense!" exclaimed Romrey, striding over. "What does it mean?"

"It means," said Obsoc, "that something on Meirjain wants people to go there."

Chapter

FOUR

Madrigo, on Boaz's last visit to Theta, had been pleased by the extent of his seeming recovery. It had almost been a trial to disabuse him.

In his memory, emblazoned there like poignant signs of an existence that might have been, Boaz saw the immense colonnades stretching to the horizon, the benign sherbet-like atmosphere fading into the crocus-colored sky. He smelled the delightful yet calming fragrances of the place. By his side walked Madrigo, that rock of assurance.

"I can see from your manner that you have proved the supremacy of mind, Boaz," he said. "You have conquered your ill fate."

"I have not conquered it," said Boaz.

And it was true. Boaz's rock-steady personality, like the modsuit he now always wore—like, on the somatic level, his strong and craggy body—was armor. Character armor, permitting him to function in the real world, but protecting a core of absolute horror.

It was Madrigo himself who had helped create this armor. Without colonnader knowledge of the mind the task would have been impossible. By the same token, it was Madrigo who was now fooled by it.

"I chose ill when I selected my names," Boaz said, "They augur a destiny I would avoid. . . ."

He spoke on, outlining his great fear. Madrigo nodded, and looked serious.

And then Boaz put his question. It would, for a fact,

have been hard to find a more audacious question. It was
the first time he had ever seen his mentor appear startled.

He waited.

"What you plan is quite impossible," said Madrigo when
he was sure he had understood Boaz's intention. "Nothing
can ever be changed. If it were otherwise, your names
would be lies."

Then Boaz knew that no human being, not even his
wise and kindly mentor, would or could help him, and the
utter loneliness of his mission overwhelmed him.

Boaz pushed the memory away, inasmuch as it could be
pushed, into the burning coffers of his mind. He had
checked the fuel rods to see that they were delivering their
energy evenly. Now he carried out a similar but less practical ritual—inspecting those parts of the ship with which
he was in somatic integration.

Apart from the space taken up by the engines, the hold,
living quarters and astrogation, there were four decks de-
voted to keeping Boaz alive. The ship was constructed on
the principle of "holistic integration," which meant that no
system in it was left entirely unaffected by what happened
in any other system. Boaz, in other words, was entirely a
part of the ship. When the engines exerted themselves, he
could feel it in his guts. When the ship changed state or
direction, he experienced a momentary feeling of vertigo.

The somatic system, as the bonemakers called it, was
all-enveloping. It extended through the walls of his living
quarters and into the working parts of the ship. Its main
bulk, however, lay in the four decks crammed with dull-
colored casings. When he moved among them, Boaz had
the feeling of moving within his own body—for this, in a
sense more real than flesh and blood, *was* his body. Even
his consciousness was maintained here.

Normal adp was silent; but this was not. Boaz did not
fully comprehend the reason why, but it whirred and
clicked in a constant mutter of mechanical conversation—although he knew it had no moving parts.

On each casing was a check screen. Moving from casing
to casing, Boaz stared in fascination at the symbols that
flickered ceaselessly on the glowing green plates. The bonemakers had taught him the meanings of some of those

symbols, though in actuality there was no need for him to look at them at all. The somatic system was entirely self-supervising.

The reason for the existence of the screens, as for his daily inspection of them, was that they constituted a reminder of where his health lay. Otherwise there was a danger (the bonemakers believed) that he might forget, and wander out of the ship's range despite the warning bleeps that would be transmitted to him were he to do so.

Last of all he went to the transmitters on the fourth level. It was an extraordinary sensation to stand there. The beams were at maximum penetration (though very nearly parallel and coherent, their strength weakened with distance due to loss of intelligibility on passing through a material medium. Each inch of emanating beam was like a computer system in its own right). Boaz had the feeling that a strong, invigorating light shone through his body, filling him with health and power.

The temptation was to spend long periods of time there, but it was a temptation he resisted every day. Quickly and efficiently he carried out his checks (to which there was a more practical point than with the processors, the transmitters being more liable to deterioration) and withdrew.

He went back to his cabin.

"Nearly there now," the ship whispered to him.

"Show me."

Boaz settled in his armchair. Dispensing with artificial displays, the ship fed his mind with an image of the Brilliancy Cluster through which he was now moving. A crimson circle pinpointed the star which it was expected would be host to the wandering planet.

Flecks of bright purple were a swarm of other ships migrating purposefully toward the same location. Some were far ahead of others—as soon as it was realized the broadcast from Brilliancy had to be genuine, they had started taking off from Sarsuce like fleas leaving a drowning dog. In the rush nobody had paused to dwell on who had sent the broadcast, or why.

"After the gold," Boaz muttered to himself. "All after the gold." It was an old saying from a time when gold had been a valuable metal and men had stampeded for any chance of laying their hands on it.

He was going to be among the stragglers getting there. There were operators in the vicinity with very fast ships, and he had delayed some hours before taking off.

But Meirjain was a big planet, and he had the advantage that he did not want as much as they did. Boaz, in his gloomy way, was feeling fairly optimistic.

The ship woke him from his troubled sleep. A minor note of urgency pervaded the summons, and Boaz came instantly to a sitting position in the armchair that served him in place of a bed.

"Look," said the ship.

Again a picture in his mind—or rather, a montage of pictures. A planet, its surface mottled purple, blue and mauve, fretted with a filigree of other colors—gold, silver, scarlet. It was warmed by a yellow sun with a hint of blue; a sun, he recognized, that offered the full spectrum of colors accessible to the human eye.

In diagramatized form he saw what the naked eye would not see: scores of ships in orbit. Their outlines flickered in his vision. Many of them he could remember seeing on Wildhart ship ground.

"Why haven't they gone down?" he asked.

"They can't," his ship told him.

"Why not?"

"I have called *The Sedulous Seeker* for you."

The Sedulous Seeker, Radalce Obsoc's yacht, was as fast as anything flying and would have been among the first vessels to arrive. Obsoc's image rose before Boaz's mind's eye, a sumptuous lounge providing a background. Mace lolled on a couch, her eyes closed.

The collector's bulging eyes glistened. "Good day, shipkeeper. You got here at last."

"What happened?" Boaz asked. "Is no one down?"

"No one has been able to get down." Obsoc's mouth twitched. "Plenty have tried. The atmosphere is impossible to penetrate."

Boaz was silent; he left it to his puzzled expression to ask the question.

"My engineer tells me the planet is surrounded by a 're-verse inertial field,' " Obsoc supplied. "Though in my view he is simply covering up ignorance with clever words."

"It doesn't make sense," Boaz said slowly.

"For Meirjain to be inaccessible? Presumably it makes sense to whatever intelligence is manipulating us in this fashion. There is something down there, shipkeeper, and it is playing games with us."

"We can't hang around here forever," Boaz said. "The cruiser will be on us in a few standard days."

"The cruiser may not *necessarily* have things all its own way. We have a regular orbital town here, Shipkeeper Boaz, and some firepower." Obsoc frowned. "The real problem is whether anything is going to come of this exercise. You may care to add your voice to an attempt to find a way out of the impasse. We are holding a meeting to see if there might be some way forward."

"Who will be at this meeting?"

"Some of those who have tried to penetrate the barrier. Also some scientific minds who are among us." Obsoc paused. "Also it has not been possible to exclude some of the more forceful personalities present. I should warn you that they are people of the most dangerous sort. Tempers are frayed; there has already been fighting."

"And who is holding it?"

"It will take place aboard my yacht. The quarters here are particularly commodious. Heave to in three standard hours if you are interested."

"All right," Boaz decided. "I'll be there."

The image disappeared from his projective imagination. "Instructions?" the ship queried.

"Continue orbit."

Boaz looked again at the planet below. For some reason the events taking place did not arouse his curiosity. He merely found the mystery annoying.

With an aggrieved sigh, he went back to sleep.

The ships were beginning to gather when Boaz approached *The Sedulous Seeker*. A crowd of them, of all shapes and sizes, stretched about the sleek, elegant form of the yacht. He recognized Romrey's natty Stardiver nestling close under the belly of the bigger spaceship, its access tube dangling. Romrey, it appeared, had already joined the party.

A voice sounded in his head, not Obsoc's but a

crewman's or else a machine's. "Citizen Obsoc welcomes you aboard, Shipkeeper Boaz."

His ship conveyed his thanks for him. He clambered down to the port, from where an access tube was already reaching out to join up with a similar tube from the star yacht. As soon as they were sealed the lid flicked up to allow him to enter.

The distance to the yacht was about fifty yards. The inertial gravity field did not operate outside the skin of the ship and once in the tube he was in free fall, pulling himself along by means of handholds. Then, as he passed the midpoint, he came down to the floor with a bump. He might have guessed, he thought ruefully, that a man as wealthy as Obsoc would have gravity even in an access tube.

The farther lid flicked up as he reached it. A solicitous robot helped him through the port. "Citizen Obsoc is in the main lounge, sir," it said, in the same voice Boaz had heard earlier. "If you will follow me."

The corridor was paneled with honeywood, an organic fibrous substance with an intriguing texture which had highlights of silver in it. A thick-piled carpet made walking a silent, mossy experience. It was quite unlike the hard though sometimes springy floors he was used to.

The robot ushered him into the lounge. Radalce Obsoc stepped politely forward to greet him.

Boaz gazed about him. Walls and ceiling were patterned in fretted gold. There was little furniture. He got the idea most of it had been removed, perhaps to make more room, perhaps to avoid risk of damage to Obsoc's valuable antiques. There were about a dozen people present, including Romrey who sat talking with a young man while a fat, bland woman watched them both. He had been invited, presumably, on the strength of the partnership the three of them had recently enjoyed. Obsoc, perhaps uniquely among those who had flocked to Wildhart, had a sense of propriety.

"You won't accommodate everybody here," he remarked.

"You refer to the ships outside? They gather like insects around honey. Word has gone around. But I have invited only twenty-six persons in all." He lowered his tone. "Over there is Larry with two of his girls. You must, of course, take care not to annoy them."

Surreptitiously he gestured to a huge man, big-boned, with the hard, aggressive face of a mobster, who stood by a table. He was flanked by two junoesque women as large as himself, younger but with a striking family resemblance—the same large-boned jaw, the flashing, challenging eyes. They would be taken for Larry's sisters or daughters. They were, Boaz knew, his clones, genetically male like himself but somatically female, having been given hormone treatment in the foetus stage. Larry's entire gang consisted of such girls, of whom he had an unknown number. Now, like most of the other guests, he stood awkwardly, impatiently sipping from a glass.

Boaz's attention was caught by the opening of another door farther along the lounge. This time it was the Hat Brothers who entered. Obsoc rushed immediately to receive them.

The Hat Brothers might also have been taken for clones, but were in fact naturally identical twins. Their appearance together was striking not so much for their look-alike features as for the black, wide-brimmed hats they both wore. The story of those metal hats was well known. Boaz was aware that the psychopathology of the professional criminal involved a passion for strong family relationships—as witness the Larry gang. The brothers' hats were welded to their skulls. Bestowed on them by their father, they were transceivers for relaying mental activity, tuned and coded only to one another. Each brother experienced all the thoughts and feelings of the other, and this had been the case since their early years. They were, in effect, one mind with two bodies.

It was an unsettling sensation to be in the presence of the brothers. Boaz watched as, walking in step, they traversed the lounge to reach the drinks table. People moved furtively out of their path. As they passed near Larry and his girls, ignoring them, there was a definite air of tension.

Deftly, like two android robots operated by a single controller, they took a drink apiece from the table top and turned to face the room.

"All right!" barked one in an acid voice. "Let's get started!"

"We're not all here yet," growled Larry, his voice testy.

"It's not our liking to be kept waiting," the Hat Brother said. Then his twin, as if continuing the same speech (which was likely pointed to the young man who had been talking with Romrey). "*You* tried to get down, and got farther than most. You're an engineer too, we hear." "And *you*," continued his brother, pointing to another man, bearded, in a crimson tunic, "you're a physicist." The twins looked around the now silent gathering. "We've enough here to be starting with. If there are any ideas, let's have them."

One of Larry's girls suddenly strode across the room. She raised her fist at the last brother to speak. "If you think you can push us around—"

"Ladies! Gentlemen! Please!" Obsoc pressed himself forward supplicatingly. "We must not quarrel. We are here to cooperate"

There was a smile of amusement hovering around Larry's thin, hard lips. He beckoned to his girl. She rejoined him.

At that moment the robot servant opened the door again. Several more people entered, including, Boaz noted to his faint surprise, a nymphgirl wearing a gauzy shift.

Obsoc turned, then reached out his arm to disengage her from the group. "May I introduce Neavy Hirester? Though you may not think it to look at her, she is an expert on inertial fields."

Looking at her, the Hat Brothers smiled ironically. "Really? Now that's something we didn't know. And where did you train, girl?"

"I didn't train," Neavy answered in a cool voice. "I had it adplanted."

"An adplant doesn't make you an *expert*," the Hat Brother said. "An *expert* is somebody who understands what he's talking about. Like my brother and I are *experts* at seeing to it that people do—"

"*Shut up, Hat,*" grated Larry. He turned to Neavy, "You've worked with fields?"

She nodded. "I was servicing generators before—"

"—you started servicing *people!*" another voice finished for her, and laughed.

Boaz wondered what urge it was that had brought the

girl to Meirjain. That she was unusual among nymph-girls—who as a rule lived only for uncomplicated sensual pleasure—was attested by her having specialist technical knowledge, albeit adplanted.

What of the others, for that matter? For her it was probably a simple desire for quick wealth, as it was with Romrey. But for some of the others—like the Hat Brothers, and the Larry Family—there had to be more to it. They were already wealthy. What kind of greedy craving was it that made them want even more wealth, at whatever risk?

Neavy was speaking. "The Meirjain barrier is quite clearly an inertial field, like the artificial gravity in a spaceship except that it resists the approach of matter instead of attracting it. And except that it's much more powerful, of course. Now it's not commonly appreciated by laymen that artificial fields of this type have a breaking point. It will be pretty high in a planet-sized field this strong, but I think we might give it a try."

"How?" Larry asked. Once she had started talking they all seemed intrigued by the idea of taking technical advice from her.

"The field is designed to keep ships out. Ergo, it will be designed to withstand any normal ship propulsion unit. So we lash up a number of units on one ship and try to go through." She paused. "I calculate that where an inertial field is used as a repulsor instead of an attractor, puncturing it will have a bubble effect. It will disintegrate—until the generator can build it up again."

"That's not an advantage," Obsoc pointed out. "It's not in our interest to clear the way for all that mob out there." He waved his hand to take in the raggle-taggle fleet gathered around his yacht.

"We won't be able to do anything about it," the girl pointed out.

Boaz spoke up. "There's another aspect to all this. The sequence of events puzzles me. A broadcast from the Wanderer practically invites us here, but then an inertial field stops us from getting down. Someone is playing games with us."

Larry pulled a face. "Nobody is there. The first expeditions reported no intelligent life. Only dead civilization."

His girls nodded approvingly, inadvertently advertising that he had already talked over this point with them.

"Then to what do you attribute both the broadcast and the field?" one of the Hat brothers asked archly.

"Some left-over machine is doing it. At random, for no reason."

"I'd say that's a good explanation," the young man Romrey had been talking to offered anxiously. His face was serious. "There used to be a saying in the Academy—when events contradict one another, put it down to nature or machine, not consciousness."

What academy he referred to wasn't clear, but his contribution was ignored as though he had never spoken. Boaz sensed something happening between Larry and the Hat brothers. He tensed, but the outcome, when it fell out, took him by surprise.

Larry looked straight at the nearest brother and raised his eyebrows. In return, both brothers nodded.

"Things need simplifying," the brother farthest from him said, though he was looking the other way and couldn't have seen Larry's signal. For a moment the three men stood motionless, eyes glazed.

"How do we do that?" the nymphgirl asked. No one seemed to have noticed the exchange between the men. The Hat brother's remark was received, with only slight bewilderment, as continuing the previous conversation.

It was, Boaz supposed, to be expected—treachery, combinations between enemies, anything that could bestow an unfair advantage even though, on the face of it, probably no one would gain anything anyway. Was Obsoc party to this, or had he innocently invited a viper to his bosom?

But what was it Larry and the Hat brothers planned? Simply to shoot down everyone present? Boaz reached out in his mind to draw extra defensive strength over the beam from his ship—but at that moment the ship itself spoke to him.

Extreme danger. Return immediately.

He was puzzled by the message. He could not imagine what threat to him there was here that the ship could not help him handle. Larry was doing nothing, merely smiling to himself, while the brothers gazed in bored fashion at the floor.

He was about to ask the ship for an explanation when a shout from the far end of the lounge directed him to the answer. A big wall screen had come on, probably activated by a robot on the yacht's bridge.

The gathered swarm of small ships was on the screen. Moving through them, firing in all directions with what looked like proton broadbeams, came two slightly larger vessels, almost certainly those belonging to the Hat brothers and to Larry and his girls.

It now became urgently clear to Boaz what the danger was. It was not directly to him. *It was to his ship.* His ship, without which he was dead. This had been prearranged; while seeming to do nothing, Larry and the Hat brothers had been sending go signals to their vessels.

The scene was little short of carnage. Very few of the starcraft had weapons, and those that were manned got under way and fled in panic. Others—mostly those whose occupants were aboard *The Sedulous Seeker*—floated passively and were junked by the withering effect of high-velocity proton pulses.

While seeing this, Boaz was on his way to the exit. There the robot which had admitted him barred his path.

"Sir, I strongly urge you not to leave the ship. It is not safe out there."

"Get out of my way!" Boaz bawled.

"Sir, for your own safety I cannot allow you to pass. Citizen Obsoc would be most distressed if you came to harm on his account."

Boaz paused, turning to see what happened in the lounge behind him. Everyone now realized what was afoot. Some recognized the identity of the attacking ships. But just as they might have been thinking of doing something about it, they were preempted by Larry's girls. Parawhips in hand, they stepped toward the gathering, their motions animal and predatory, sending the thin whips singing out warningly over the heads of those present.

The Hat brothers entered into the act, too. Producing numbnerve guns, they spearated to dance down opposite sides of the lounge. Watching them move was fascinating. It was not a walk, not a lope, but more like a beautifully coordinated balletic performance. Boaz realized that they

enjoyed moving together. *Phut, phut* went the hazy blue
spheres of static they sent rebounding through the lounge
from the muzzles of their guns, again taking care not to
aim at anyone.

"Don't anybody move," said a brother in a confident,
low-timbred voice. "When we've cleared the riffraff away
we'll carry out the nymphgirl's plan."

"My ship!" screamed someone. Boaz waited to see no
more. He pushed aside the robot, who did not have the
strength to restrain a human being anyway, and ran down
the corridor.

Others had got the idea of trying to save their craft by
the time he reached the skin of the ship, but he had no
difficulty in sending the signal that automatically reconnect-
ed the access tubes. Wondering what he would do if a
proton beam accidentally sliced through the tunnel, he
hauled himself swiftly along it and in minutes had re-
gained his own ship.

As with most vessels, there was no external armament
and it was imperative to get out of danger as quickly as
possible. Ordering the ship to bring him an image of surrounding space, he went to his cabin.

The long shaft of Obsoc's yacht floated fifty yards away.
In the other direction was a scene of chaos. With scarcely
a thought from Boaz, the ship disconnected and was about
to withdraw the access tube, when he noticed a figure
floating near the dangling end of another access tube farther along *The Sedulous Seeker*.

The figure, wearing an emergency space cape and twisting slowly, looked familiar. "Give me a closer look at
that," Boaz ordered.

The picture zoomed in his mind. As he had thought, it
was Romrey. Panning the image, Boaz found the wreck of
his *Stardiver*. Romrey must have been trying to reach it,
and had somehow fallen out of the end of the tube. Very
careless of him.

Boaz knew he should be steering his ship away from
here without delay. But there was never a time when ethics could be entirely overridden. He nudged the ship closer
and ordered the tube extended toward the stranded man.

Suddenly the ship spoke to him again, with a note of

even greater urgency. *Attention. A government cruiser approaches.*

"What?" Boaz spoke out loud in his startlement. "But it isn't due for another two standard days."

Whoever made that assessment was mistaken, or mischievous. It is here.

"Let me see."

From a purely rational point of view the ensuing images were confusing, but Boaz was used to the semi-diagrammatic way of representation his ship sometimes adopted. He saw Romrey reaching for the access tube, ridiculously waving his arms and legs as though swimming toward it (like most people, he had practically no experience of free fall). He saw the scattering, damaged cloud of spacecraft, as though from a different viewpoint imposed on the first. And imposed on *that*, he saw the fully armed econosphere cruiser, more than twice as large as Obsoc's yacht, its form functional and ungainly—ugly, in fact—swiftly moving in to enforce the government edict which everyone here had defied.

The montage fused into one coherent picture as the cruiser darted sharklike among the still-disorganized crowd of ships, the official blazon—a starburst with eight glowing rays—clearly visible on its flanks. The servants of the econosphere were notoriously unfastidious about how they achieved their aims. The cruiser opened fire from the start, ruthlessly selecting targets with a view to chasing away anyone trying to land on the planet that loomed to one side of the scene. Its heavy-duty beams immediately vaporized three ships. Its staff was probably surprised, however, to see the eerie blue glow of a magnetic defense screen abruptly surround *The Sedulous Seeker*. The yacht returned fire and began to accelerate, sliding around the gorgeous curve of Meirjain.

The two ships that earlier had been firing on the assembly followed suit—presumably because Larry and the Hat Brothers were still aboard Obsoc's yacht. They, too, opened up on the now pursuing cruiser. In seconds all four vessels had disappeared over the horizon.

But they would soon be back. "Seal the tube and haul it in quickly," Boaz ordered. "This is all a dead loss. We shall have to withdraw."

It is being done, the ship said. Then: *A message is coming through. Listen.*

Once again a set of interpreted images impinged on Boaz's consciousness. When the crowd of ships scattered in panic, one of them had gone plunging down toward the planet. Now, from within the atmosphere, an excited voice was broadcasting from that ship.

"The screen is down. I'm getting through! The screen's vanished, everybody! I'm going right on down!"

Wryly Boaz reflected that the broadcaster was doing himself little good by making this announcement. Probably he had been betrayed by a sudden excess of enthusiasm and a misplaced sense of camaraderie with his fellow prospectors. But whoever he was, Boaz felt grateful for his mistake. A note of triumph entered his feelings.

Your guest is aboard, the ship informed him.

"Take us down," Boaz said. "We're landing on Meirjain."

Chapter

FIVE

The descent had been hasty, the need to escape the enforcer cruiser's ravening beams overriding any interest Boaz felt in the enlarging landscape. The cruiser, shooting ships out of the sky as it came back round the curve of the planet, *The Sedulous Seeker* fleeing before it, had followed the mob as far as the troposphere—before returning again to orbit. *The Sedulous Seeker* and its two sudden allies, the armed ships belonging to Larry and the Hat Brothers, had soon abandoned their abortive attempt to put the cruiser out of action and, outgunned, had also dived into the atmosphere.

Vast patches of gold and silver, interspersing a less brilliant background of lavender and violet, had slid past below. The prospectors, including Boaz, had all made an instinctive dash for darkness, zipping in a drove over the terminator before scattering. In fact the cruiser would be able to scan the night as well as the day, and for that matter probably had orders not to fire on the surface of Meirjain. But people felt safer in the dark. Boaz, like the others, sought cover, landing in what looked like the leeward side of a cliff.

No one would move until daylight came. Boaz calculated that the hours of waiting would be useful, putting the commander of the government cruiser in a more passive mode. He would probably take no further action until the prospector ships tried to leave the planet—then their problems would begin in earnest.

Boaz reminisced, skulking within his ship.

"What you plan is quite impossible. Nothing can ever be changed."

These words of Madrigo, uttered at Boaz's last meeting with him, were often replayed in the shipkeeper's mind. They dropped into his consciousness now, provoking as usual a response that he knew was perverse. They should have affected him like drops of slow poison, steadily depressing him into senselessness. Instead, they infected him with a kind of manic exhilaration. Insane stubbornness, irrational determination, gave his will a hard edge. When last had man pitted himself against the gods?

Romrey sat watching Boaz curiously from the other side of the small cabin. The shipkeeper had rebuffed all his attempts to engage in conversation. He sat slouched over a table, moodily fondling his deck of colonnader cards while waiting for Meirjain's new sun to come up. The totality of his self-absorption reminded Romrey of someone on a run-up to suicide—*real* suicide, not clone-backed self-immolation.

What *was* it, he wondered, that Boaz was after? He gestured to the cards. "You have a deck, too. Are they anything like mine?"

Boaz shook his head. "Nothing like," he muttered. Actually Romrey would have found little difference, but for Boaz there was no comparison. In his cards the symbolism was pure and elegant, with none of the carborundum deck's florid arcanery. They were philosophical, not occult. Neither did he expect any mysterious help from them, as Romrey did from his.

He stopped at the card called the Universe. One way in which the colonnader cards differed from the degraded decks was that however familiar the images became they seemed fresh and new each time one looked at them. Boaz could still intuit original nuances, even after years of study.

The Universe showed a city set on an island, amid a wavy blue-green sea. Gaily-garbed people thronged the balconies, traversed the walkways, ascended and descended the upthrusting towers, appeared briefly at countless windows. The meaning of the card was relatively simple (though a wealth of more technical ideas was encoded in the shapes and numbers of its towers and shafts). It expressed the basic colonnader idea that the universe was an organized whole, and that all sentient beings in it were, so to speak, citizens of a common *polis*.

Boaz thumbed out two more cards: the Priestess, which was the Universe's complementary card at the other end of the twenty-one card sequence, and Strength, which as the middle pivotal card of the whole sequence linked them together. The three cards comprised a potent triad. The Priestess was a card of ceaseless allure and enchantment. She sat on a throne, smiling in benign, pleased fashion at the beholder. The pillars *Joachim* and *Boaz* flanked her rear, the space between them screened by a veil merging with the wimple she wore as a headdress. On her lap lay an open book, whose pages she turned one by one, unendingly. Each leaf of this book, the reverse of which was left blank, bore exactly the same image: a miniature of the card called the Universe. It was complete in every detail, every tower, ever traverse, every citizen, every tiny motion. Again and again the city reappeared, absolutely unvarying from page to page, vanishing for the moment that the leaf was turned.

Thus was the doctrine of the world's eternal recurrence explicated.

Strength, the card through which the other two interacted was also a female card. A willowy woman, wearing a flowing gown, stood on a bare landscape. Her face was serene and gentle. In her two hands she held the jaws of a lion, which somehow seemed to merge with or emerge from her pelvis.

Some called the card Nature, or the Strength of Nature. Others Force, or Conservation. Few without colonnader training knew what it really signified: the obdurate rock-steadiness of natural forces, which were absolutely self-regulating in the cosmic context, and which could not be made to swerve or alter by a single iota.

Madrigo had explained: "Imagine a force which whenever it acts calls into play a countervailing force which instantly dampens it down. Such a force would display no positive characteristic, and would be undetectable. It would be indistinguishable from empty void. And yet it might be nature's ultimate force that maintains all others.

"Such a force exists. It is indeed the ultimate conserving force, the absolute bedrock of nature. It cannot be detected. Neither can it be interfered with, even in the least degree. . . ."

Boaz laid out the three cards in a triangle. Here was the Priestess, the birth of the universe when the twin pillars of existence separated from one another and matter unfolded from potentiality, just like a book opening. Here was the Universe: the world-city itself, no more than a detail in the Priestess. And here, at the other corner of the triangle, was Strength, the linking card. This explained, to the superior understanding, why it was that the world could only exist in the mode of eternal repetition, for otherwise there would be no unity to nature, no strength. . . .

The cards distressed him and he rose from the occasional table where he had been seated, to go pacing about the narrow space.

Eternal recurrence . . . it was his burden. Should it not be everyone's? What was more depressing than that one's life must be repeated endlessly, to the last unalterable syllable? . . . But to₄ the common man this knowledge had no meaning, he realized. It was an equation in a book. Only to a philosopher, to Boaz who had had the sure proof of the equation shown to him, for whom it had become a part of everyday thought, was it as real as yesterday, tomorrow, or today.

His stricken look amazed Romrey. He stared up at the shipkeeper. "What's wrong?" he asked. "Did you see something in the cards?"

"If you like," Boaz answered brusquely.

"You know," Romrey said, after a thoughtful pause, "it's probably not good manners after you saved my life, but I'm curious about you. You look like one lonely man to me."

Words came from Boaz before he had time to check them. "Loneliness: an abyss without a bottom, into which to fall without limit. So it must be."

The intensity of Boaz's pronouncement took Romrey aback slightly. "Nobody need be that alone," he said. "I wonder if you'd mind telling me what you're hoping to find here on the Wanderer. It's probably not money, like the rest of us."

When Boaz ignored him, he slipped his carborundum cards out of his pocket. "Well, maybe *these* can tell me," he said, and began to shuffle preparatory to dealing them out for a reading.

He had half feared that Boaz would react to his temerity by turning him out onto the surface to fend for himself, regardless of colonnader ethics. Boaz, indeed, seemed angry. He knocked the cards from Romrey's hand.

"This trash will tell you nothing." He spoke thickly. "Your pack has not the depth. Very well, you importuning thief, I will tell you. Who knows, perhaps you have the intelligence to understand it. But first you must be able to understand that there could be a man who has suffered in a way unknown by any other being in the history of creation. Could you believe in inconceivable suffering? Does it sound like a melodramatic exaggeration? No, it is literally true, and I am that man. I will not explain how, except to say that science, in seeking greater good, has wrought the greatest ever evil, and that the school of mental calm is responsible for such agony as to make calm impossible. All my actions are directed toward escaping from this agony. And that is why I am on Meirjain."

"You suffer it *now?*" Romrey inquired.

"It is in the past." Boaz turned away to hide his haunted eyes.

"Then you already have escaped it," Romrey said, puzzled. He shrugged. "If the memory is unbearable, you could always have it erased."

"No!" Boaz turned to Romrey again. His expression was savage. "Don't you see? The universe repeats. Everything that has gone before must come again, and again, forever and ever. It lies before me."

"Yes, of course," muttered Romrey, though he showed by his quizzical expression that the idea was barely comprehensible to him.

Suddenly he laughed softly. "It *is* time-gems you're after, then! You want time travel, right? To travel back and change what happened . . . whatever it was. . . ."

"The past? Why change the past?" Boaz shook his head. "You disappoint me, Gare. Do you know nothing of cosmology? *The future is the past.* Because the future has already occurred, countless times in the past. What has been must be, again and again. Do you see, Gare? *What has been must be, again and again.* I must change the *future*, abolish predestination, put time on a new track."

"Past, present or future, everybody knows time is immutable—predestined, as you put it. The world goes from phase to phase of the same eternal cycle. It's a law."

"Time has been immutable till *now*." Boaz slammed his fist on the table, causing the cards he had lain there to jump. "You are wrong. It is not a law. It is a circumstance. Nature is strong, but not omnipotent. Indeed, her strength can be used against her."

It was on this point that all his hopes were pinned. He had studied all the data obtained by scientists, and all the arguments of the philosophers, and he had concluded that nothing made predestination an absolute law. It was a consequence of the strength of nature, that was all. The sheer weight of the universe, so to speak, caused events to run an identical course with each manifestation. If someone could be strong enough, or clever enough. . . .

"If one small detail in present time can be altered," he went on, "then eventually all will be altered. The tiniest deviation can only accumulate, until there are untold results." His voice shook. "If only somewhere in the whole vast universe, some little flower can be caused to have seven petals instead of eight! If one lone electron orbit acquires one quantum of energy more or less! Then the next manifestation of the world will not be identical to this one, and the next one will be different again. The nature of cause and effect must make it so. Then," he added dreamily, "my prison will be shattered. I shall have a chance to be spared that torment."

"It might mean you don't exist at all, next time," Romrey ruminated.

"Gladly, gladly!"

"Mankind might not exist either."

"What does it matter? Conceivably the whole universe will never exist again. There might be just nothing, forever and ever. Or it might take a wholly new form, in which matter itself will be different. I do not care one jot about it. All I care is that—"

Boaz halted, his fist clenched. A knowing look had come over Romrey's face. He spread his legs so that the colonnader cards that Boaz had knocked on the floor became visible.

The cards had fallen in a mass facesdown. Only one card had separated and lay face up. Romrey bent and retrieved it. It pictured a stone tower in the instant of being shattered by a massive lightning bolt or gush of energy. From its buckling height a lone figure tumbled head first.

Romrey said sourly, "So we have a reading after all. This card is something of a mystery. There's no general agreement on its meaning. Some people call it 'the Universe Buster.' If that's right, you've interpreted it nicely."

Staring at the card, Boaz said, "It symbolizes simultaneous creation and destruction, in the colonnader deck."

They fell silent. How Sisyphean, Boaz wondered for the thousandth time, was his task? The time-gems gave some prospect of hope—yet how often had he spent his life in this quest, only for the rock of his labors to roll back down to its resting place at his death?

In a sense, he was forced to admit that the hopelessness of his quest was the very essence of it. Its audacity, its irrational grandiosity, gave point to his existence. He pursued only because life offered no other possibility. . . .

Romrey, meanwhile, was having thoughts of his own. He knew now, after what he had just heard, that Joachim Boaz was quite insane.

Together, without speaking, they waited for the dawn.

It came first as a glow that suffused the darkness, then as a sudden blaze. Surveying the scene through the ship's sensors, Boaz saw at once that he had misjudged his surroundings when landing in the darkness, but he decided that the ship might as well stay put for the present. The atmosphere checked as breathable, just as previous explorers had reported—though as a different sun had then warmed the planet, the datum was not necessarily reliable.

Boaz got busy, getting together a tool kit and float sledge. "If you like, we'll go together."

Romrey nodded.

"We'll make a short reconnoitre to start with," Boaz continued. "As you may have guessed, there is a limit to how far I can wander from my ship. You may be useful to me in that regard."

No mist rose from the ground to greet the burgeoning yellow sun as they descended the tread-rail. The air was perfectly clear, the landscape shining. The sky was like none either man had ever seen: it seemed to be of no single color, but glimmered patchily, mauve, blue, pink, shot through with channels and outlines of brighter colors, like a reflection of the planet's surface as it had appeared from space—which it probably was, thought Boaz, wondering what combination of upper atmosphere gases might bring about such a refractive trick.

But it was the ground below that held the greatest surprise. It was not ground but a floor, stretching indistinctly toward the horizon. It shone, it gleamed, it was brilliant but with a soft brilliance. It was pure yellow. As soon as they set foot on it Boaz took a cutting tool from his kit. In moments he had cut out a cavity in which yellow shadows gleamed. Wonderingly he massaged in his hands the lump he had cut. It was so malleable he could bend it where it was not too thick, needing to summon only a little strength over his integration beam.

He tested the metal with a chemical assay. Gold. Purest gold. The plain was made of it. Now that he looked closer he could see that it was marked with a checkerboard of fine, barely visible etched lines.

Romrey eyed the sample without interest. Though neither of them had ever seen gold used so lavishly, it was, like every other natural element except radium and technetium, too low in value to be worth taking. What everyone now scattered around Meirjain was after was the incredibly rare, the new, the unexpected, small in bulk and huge in desirability—like time-gems. . . .

Boaz threw aside the lump and directed Romrey's attention to what, on landing, he had taken to be an uneven cliff wall behind them.

It was not a cliff wall. It was definitely artificial. It was a bulging, rounded hull, reddish gold in hue but studded and decorated with baroque traceries the color of ruby, cobalt, copper and amber. The two men were too close to the gigantic structure to gain any clear idea of its nature, and Boaz gestured to Romrey to mount the float sled. Together they glided over the gold floor for a distance of about a mile.

Looking back, it was just possible to see what the "cliff" was. It was, Boaz was sure, a ship, though conceivably it might have been a fixed building of fantastic shape. But what a ship! No econosphere spacedock, nor the yards of any past or present civilization in Boaz's ken, had ever constructed or planned a vessel remotely like it in size and magnificence. Its height was about a mile, but it rested lengthways on immense ornate runners, and its length was about three miles. Its form was everywhere gently rounded, though its sides, as near as Boaz could judge, were nearly parallel near the center. As the sun rose, at an angle to the horizon, the light slid along the shining bulk disclosing a richness of age, and of sheer wealth.

And that was not all. On either side of it were similar ships, forming a rank from horizon to horizon. This was a parking ground.

"By the gods," Romrey muttered. "Just look at that. I wonder if the other people who came to the Wanderer found anything like this?"

"There's no saying. Most information about what was found here was suppressed. Not that there seems to have been all that much of it in the first place. They only stayed a few hours."

"Yeah, I know. A slingshot orbit. When they came back, Meirjain was gone and they never tracked it again—until now. Phew." A greedy look came over Romrey's face. "We've got to get inside one of those things."

"Later, perhaps," frowned Boaz. He was looking in the opposite direction. Near the horizon, which was about three miles away, was a different type of structure. It looked rather like a miniature city built of purple blocks, towers and various other shapes that were indistinct at this distance. Although it could have been an industrial plant or some such artifact, it did have more of the appearance of a permanent dwelling than the monstrous vessels—although, paradoxically, it also seemed smaller.

"That might be a better place to look, at first," he observed.

He was about to put the sledge in motion again when Romrey gave an alarmed grunt and pointed to the sky. Limned against the confusing multicolored backdrop was a

slender shape, which as they watched enlarged itself into
the elegant outline of Radalce Obsoc's yacht. Boaz stayed
his hand on the controls of the float sledge. *The Sedulous
Seeker* hovered, moved to and fro slightly, then put down
not half a mile away.

"What do you think?" Romrey asked. "This isn't coincidence."

"Not with a whole planet to fly to."

"I'm not going to like it if all those people are aboard.
Especially you-know-who."

Boaz was prepared to deal mortally with the persons
Romrey referred to, if he had to. He decided it was an issue best faced up to now rather than left until later. He
put the sledge on a steady glide and swept toward the por-
tal of the yacht. It opened even before they reached it.

Obsoc appeared in the entrance as they stepped off the
sledge. He was blinking rapidly and his face showed obvious strain. "Oh, come in, come in, both of you," he en-
treated in a high-pitched voice. "You don't know how glad
I am to see you. It's been simply dreadful."

"Are the others with you?" Boaz asked him.

"Ach!" Obsoc put his hand to his forehead. "Only
Neavy. And I think she's dying."

He led them into the main lounge. Neavy Hirester lay
on a couch, attended by one of the yacht robots which
had been given a medical program. Mace was kneeling
beside her, a hand on her brow.

No one else was present in the lounge. Boaz noticed,
however, the dark bloodstains on the carpet.

He and Romrey stepped near the couch. Neavy's eyes
were closed, and she appeared unconscious. She was very
pale. Her clothing was open and the robot was binding an
ugly cut with a surgical instrument.

"It isn't really any use," Mace said, glancing up. "She's
lost too much blood, and we haven't got any."

"What did it?"

"Parawhips. Those damned girls. She's got some really
deep lacerations. Hemorrhaged like mad."

Boaz turned to Obsoc. "How did you find us?"

"My robots tracked you down. I hope you don't mind
our turning up like this. I feel shaken, citizens, I don't
mind telling you—what a business?"

"What happened?" asked Romrey.

"As soon as they realized the barrier was down Larry and the Hat Brothers started fighting. They just didn't care—they were killing anyone. They would have killed us too, if our robots hadn't helped us to hide. One of Larry's girls was killed, too. Luckily their own ships came down for them, and they left."

"You mean everyone else is dead, except Neavy?"

Obsoc nodded. "Everyone. Oh, what a business! The carnage!"

"Where are the bodies?"

"I got the robots to throw them out." Obsoc rubbed his eyes, as if very tired, then leaned against a table. "This is dreadful. What am I doing here? I have risked my life—for what? For the satisfaction of ownership! And yet I would do it again. My friends, you probably do not understand these things. You cannot comprehend the compulsion that comes over the impassioned collector."

"It is the same as any other vice," Boaz said absently. "The object of it is largely irrelevant." He reflected. "You haven't seen anything more of the econosphere ship?"

"No. It won't bother us while we're down here."

"I think she's going," Mace said sadly.

The robot paused, then felt a pulse, probed for a heartbeat, and finally applied a little flat meter box to the girl's temple. It straightened.

"She has died, sir," it said to Obsoc.

Obsoc sighed, a trifle ostentatiously. "All right, put her outside."

Romrey stirred. "I don't think I like the idea of a corpse lying around the place."

"Oh, all right." Obsoc gestured to the robot. "Put her in the freezer. You can dispose of her later." The robot bent and, with obvious difficulty (robots generally were quite frail), lifted the dead girl in its arms and carried her out.

"I wonder if she has a clone," Mace said dreamily. "The trouble is, it's probably light-years away. It won't receive her death signal."

The men ignored her. Obsoc's manner suddenly changed and became brisk as he spoke to the other two. "Well, gentlemen, from the look of it you were about to do some exploring. You've noticed those gigantic ships, I suppose?

From the air you can see hundreds of them! And that's not all. This planet is a fairyland. It's quite unbelievable. How the race that did all this could have died out I just don't know."

"We were heading for the citylike structure," Boaz said. "I suppose you have a suggestion to make?"

Obsoc shrugged. He looked uncertain, and Boaz realized that he was frightened. He wanted the other two to find the goods for him.

"Perhaps we can be most useful to one another when it comes to leaving," Boaz offered. "There is still the cruiser to be got past."

"And the time-gems?" Obsoc queried anxiously.

"If we find any, we'll share them."

"Good! And if there should be other finds—other jewels, hitherto unknown, perhaps—"

"We'll have to talk about it," Romrey said sourly. "Maybe you'll have to do some exploring yourself." He turned to the exit. "Well, how about it, shipkeeper? We're wasting time."

They left. Outside, Boaz put the sledge in motion again, and they set off for their goal. As they came closer, some first impressions of the "city" were dispelled. On the one hand it began to seem more machinelike, the blocks and pipes taking on the appearance of components of a mechanism. On the other, the purple color resolved itself into a pointillism of colors which glittered like tinsel, all merging at a distance into the one luminous purple. There was an eerie beauty to it that threatened to befuddle the senses—or at least Boaz thought so. From the restlessness of his companion he guessed that Romrey was simply filling himself with excited thoughts of riches.

A low wall, about three feet in height, surrounded the city. He floated the sledge over it, then set down and stepped out, looking around him. He touched the wall; it had a roughened surface, every wrinkle of which was a different color. He was not surprised at the apparently perfect state of preservation of what they had seen so far. Only primitive civilizations built with materials that decayed. It was another question whether the long-dead inhabitants had left behind them any energy sources that were also non-degradable. If so, it was remotely possible that even the ships looming behind them were still workable.

Neither was it the first time that Boaz had stood amid the works of an alien culture. His search for a means to change time had led him to many strange places. He lifted his gaze and surveyed what turned out to be a tangle of pylons, snaking pipelike shapes, oddly formed blocks, figures from some twisted geometry.

"There's something queer about this place," Romrey said.

"I know what you mean." Boaz picked on a spot and tried to follow a pipe, oval in cross-section, as it veered among the towers of the "city." He soon lost it.

There was a topological oddness to it all. While it obviously existed in the normal three dimensions of space, it reminded him more than anything of sketches and models that were meant to represent forms in four-dimensional space. The thought gave him a feeling of excitement that subjectively, he guessed, was much like Romrey's delirium of greed for wealth.

He looked back. His ship was a small grey shape against the golden balloon of the Meirjain giant. It was already some miles away, and there was no saying whether there might not be materials in the "city" that would prove impervious to its beams, or at least that might attenuate them. He issued a silent command: *Follow*. Obediently the ship lifted itself, soared past *The Sedulous Seeker* (which unlike Boaz's ship had a horizontal landing attitude) and put down half a mile away.

Romrey observed the move in silence. "Let's move," Boaz said. "If we find any doors, we might be able to tell what kind of place this is."

Romrey stepped down from the sledge, which dutifully trailed after them as they moved deeper into the "city." Soon it engulfed them. The sky seemed to disappear, its colors merging with those of the structures that rose and danced all around them. His surroundings began to seem forbidding to Boaz. He was telling himself that they were wasting their time here, and that they would do better to search elsewhere, when a cry of "Hey!" came from Romrey.

He had found an entrance to one of the blocklike buildings, shaped like a man-sized door. The aperture was too small to admit the sledge. Leaving it parked outside, Boaz followed his companion through.

Inside, the darkness was almost complete. Boaz switched on a torch and held it aloft. By its fierce radiance he saw that they were in an empty chamber, cube-shaped but with rounded corners. In the opposite wall was another entrance, this time oval but also of a size to admit a man.

Romrey peered through it. "It's a tunnel."

Boaz joined him, twisting the ring on the torch to produce a beam. There was nothing to be seen in the tunnel, which after a few yards curved out of sight.

Pausing, Boaz told himself that poking into any chance corner was perhaps not the best way of persuading this fabled world to reveal its treasures. A more reliable method might be to trust his ship's spy beams. While Romrey urged him to go down the tunnel, he summoned up the ship, asking which way he should go.

The ship spoke, but mingled with the message was a note that was unfamiliar. *Go forward*.

He stepped through the opening, beckoning Romrey to follow.

They moved cautiously, for what seemed a long time. There was no apparent sense to the oval corridor's convolutions: it turned this way and that, it dipped, it rose, it slanted at random oblique angles, it turned—so Boaz suspected—back on itself. Then, as he was about to suggest they retrace their steps, it delivered them to a low-ceilinged, boat-shaped chamber, about the size of the lounge in Radalce Obsoc's yacht.

Returning the torch to an all-round lamp, he took quick stock of the room. The walls were of a matt lavender louvred with close-set ribs which followed the curve of the chamber like the ribs of a sail-driven water boat. Placed along the center of the chamber were about half a dozen closed chests, or coffers. A storage place, perhaps?

Romrey dashed to the chests and threw open the unresisting lid of the first one he came to. He drew his breath in sharply, dipped in a hand and pulled out something that glittered.

It looked at first like a silver spider's web. But its threads seemed to flow and reorganize themselves constantly as Romrey held it up to the light, turned it over and examined it through an eyeglass.

"I don't know what this stuff is. Never seen anything like it before."

Boaz was not listening to him. He was receiving a message, which at first he thought came from his ship—but no, it was that other, unfamiliar note which minutes before had mingled with the ship's voice.

Here, little Mudworm, is the treasure you seek.

Mudworm! That hated name—the name he had not heard all these years, the original name he had been given by his enemies—where had it come from now? What was speaking to him?

With the words, there was an instruction. He was directed to the third chest in the row. Moving to it, he saw that it had a transparent lid. Not only that, but a square in the ceiling over it was also transparent, and light—daylight, as far as he could tell—shone down onto the cask below.

Through the crystalline lid, he saw a layer of what appeared to be large diamonds.

The use of his earlier name had provoked turbulent and unpleasant feelings in Boaz. Nevertheless he forced himself to be calm, and lifted the lid.

The gems, about a hundred of them, were laid on something resembling velvet. Each was faceted, and about an inch and a half in diameter. Boaz picked one up, turned it over, let it catch the light.

Romrey was suddenly at his elbow, the silver spider web dangling from his hand. "What's that? Is it . . .?"

For answer, Boaz brought the gem close to his face to peer into it. One could see reflections in the facets, tiny little pictures. He brought it closer to his eye, looking as though through a lens.

And he saw himself and Romrey, coasting over the yellow plain on the float sledge, reaching the "city," dismounting. . . .

A scene from the recent past.

Now he understood why this chest had a transparent lid, why the light shone on it from outside. Time-gems refracted light through time. From the past, from the future. The overhead panel brought it light from the city's environs.

But a scene from the past could be explained by other means than time transference. He turned to another facet. And saw himself again.

He saw Romrey, too, but something was wrong. Romrey was standing like a statue, staring ahead of him as if frozen. In the scene Boaz himself seemed disturbed. He staggered, peered close at Romrey, reached out his arm to touch him. . . .

The picture faded.

A warning?

"What did you see?" asked Romrey. He reached past Boaz and picked up another gem, focusing his gaze into it as Boaz had done. For a while both men were absorbed in the tiny picture shows.

It was strange that images so minuscule, and presumably bounced around the interiors of the gems at random, should be so clear. The gems themselves were as limpid as water, except where glints and sparkles flashed through them—and as these glints enlarged themselves, as the facets were turned, the scenes came suddenly into focus, never lasting more than a few seconds before vanishing.

If the glimpses were all from past and future time, then the range was immense; somehow Boaz had expected it to encompass a few hours or minutes only—perhaps no more than seconds or a part of a second. Briefly he saw a perfect little landscape with a yellow sun and wavy, frondlike trees swishing over dusty ground. Flowerlike creatures walked in groups beneath those trees. . . . Now he saw one of the golden ships flying. It swept over Meirjain's fantastic landscape, then soared upward, disappearing in a sky that was blue rather than mottled.

Boaz snatched up another gem and examined it for scenes also. He was greedy for evidence of time transference. But fascinating though the little cameos were, nothing seemed to distinguish one jewel from another.

"Let's get 'em," Romrey exclaimed feverishly. They scooped the gems up, pouring them into their belt pouches. Then Romrey turned his attention to the other chests.

Boaz stood where he was. He had retained the last gem in his hand and was staring into it. He turned the stone ever so slightly, until a tiny scene came into focus.

For the first time the scene was within the chamber itself. The six chests were being carried into it and laid down in a row, just as he and Romrey had found them. The work was being done by humanoid, olive-skinned creatures who were completely naked except for silver circlets around their waists. The humanish impression was completely destroyed, however, by their faces, which more than anything resembled the head of an Egyptian ibis. . . .

It was wholly coincidence, a startled Boaz decided, that the ibis also figured in a colonnader card entitled the Stellar Realm. . . .

He tried to hold the scene, but his fingers trembled and he lost it.

He dropped the gem in his pouch.

He felt frightened. He did not know who or what had spoken to him a short while ago. He presumed it was a thought from his own mind (perhaps even some sinister stray datum from his ship?); he wanted to stay and explore further, at the same time fighting an urge to leave, now, with what he had found.

What happened next was terrifying, yet so unexpected and bewildering that, paradoxically, it was robbed of its terror. He was seized. He felt something pick him up and *move* him, like a chess piece. He hurtled up the winding tunnel, *which was still lit by the beam of his torch.* An astonishing flurry of sights, thoughts, words and sensations dizzied past him.

He stood in the lounge of Obsoc's yacht. "Perhaps we can be most useful to one another when it comes to leaving," he said to the anxious collector. "There is still the cruiser to be got past."

"And the time-gems?"

"If we find any, we'll share them round."

"Good!" Obsoc's eyes gleamed. "And if there should be other finds—"

Once again the chess piece was moved from square to square. Boaz was picked up, whisked across the board. Flashing squares of yellow gold. A kaleidoscope of impressions, like a vid recording played a hundred times too fast. The jewel chamber. Purple blocks. Words, feelings. Flashing squares of yellow gold.

He stood in the lounge of Obsoc's yacht. He spoke to
one of the yacht robots. "Take off and enter circumpolar
orbit, achieving stable velocity over the magnetic north
pole. Meanwhile broadcast a surrender message to the
government cruiser. With luck they will intercept you
rather than shoot you down, and you can gain medical assistance for your master and his friends."

The robot inclined its head in understanding. Boaz
turned to go, and in turning was moved off again, even
faster than before. He was in the storage chamber.
Romrey had stuffed his pouches full and shook loose a
carry-bag, which he also proceeded to fill.

"This is where they kept their valuables, all right. I
don't recognize a single gem-stone, not a single metal—if
they are metals. Come on, get your share."

"Let's go."

"Go?"

Boaz was mad with elation. "I knew it was true," he
murmured. Already he understood that he had traveled
through time, to the past, then to the future, and now
back to the present. "The answer is here."

But he felt a terrible fear that whatever power it was
that had seized him would carry him out of the range of
his ship's healing beams. That would be the end of him—
in the agony he was doing all this to avoid.

"I'm going back to the ship," he said. "Do what you
like."

"Well, all right. But let's get a couple of these chests to
the sledge."

"I'm going straight back." Boaz turned and started back
up the tunnel. Twisting and turning, he eventually gained
the outside, to find that Romrey was not far behind him.

"What's the matter with you?" Romrey said. "We were
doing fine."

Boaz ignored him and made his way through the complex's eye-straining shapes, signing the sledge to follow.
There was a fact that up to now he had been too numbed
to admit, but that now was bursting upon him.

It was as if the unreality of a dream had imposed itself
on real experience, and as in a dream logic had been
short-circuited. But now logic was back, bringing with it a
single, luminous inference. *Meirjain was not uninhabited.*

He had been projected into his past, then into his future, he presumed (in the hastiness of his thought he found no time to wonder what was implied by his future instructions to the yacht robot). Ergo, beings existed here who had mastered time travel, probably the same ibis-headed beings he had seen in the time-gem.

Unless a machine had accomplished it, acting at random? Possible, he thought, but unlikely.

Romrey joined him as he stepped over the wall and turned his back on the complex. They saw that a third prospector ship had landed on the plain, a little way in front of his own. Like *The Sedulous Seeker* it was horizontal in line, but much smaller and sleeker.

"I don't like this," Romrey breathed. "That's the Hat Brothers' ship."

And even as he spoke the figures of the two brothers were already emerging, distinctive in their dark garments and wide-brimmed hats. Romrey came abreast of Boaz, who stood still. "They must have followed Obsoc here," he said. "They probably imagine he knows something they don't about time-gems."

"Fools," Boaz muttered. "The time-gems are all over the planet. How else could we have found them so easily?"

Giving a nervous smile, Romrey took his deck of cards out of a pocket. "You are too skeptical, shipkeeper. It was these cards that led us to the gems. They create events, remember? I told you they were effective."

"Don't you know the econosphere regulates against magic charms?" Boaz replied acidly. "Never mind. I will deal with the Hat Brothers. Come along."

He had meant to move off toward *The Sedulous Seeker*. But before he could take the first step a sensation like a sudden and crushing blow made him gasp and stagger. It was as if a huge shadow stood over him, as if a great weight, a gigantic foot, were stamping down to crush him like an insect. And yet the blow was not physical at all. It was mental, a blow at his consciousness.

He gave a choking cry. Instantly the ship was coming to his aid. He felt the integrative machinery gearing up, reaching out, casting about for the source of the attack. Briefly he had the peculiar sensation of being frozen in a block of ice. Then a titanic struggle, an unbearable tension, permeated his body. It was total war, interspersed, to his amazement, with fragmentary, whispered comments.

"*Special measures necessary. . . . Total opposition. . . . The impact has radius vectors in the negative dimension. . . .*"

He was hearing the ship talking to itself as it sought to save him! Never before had he experienced *that!* On and on the voices went, debating, conferring, deciding—and all, he realized later, in a split second of time. Then a moment of horror as the ship, as if demoralized, consulted him:

"*You may submit, if you wish.*"

"*No!*" Boaz shouted. He knew in his heart that it would be the end of him if he surrendered to the assault. He felt the ship rally and try again. He staggered once more, forgot where he was for an instant, and then was suddenly still.

It was over, except for a feeling of inner pressure which betokened an extra vigilance from the ship.

Apart from that, what had changed?

Romrey had changed. The prospector stood stock-still, like a statue. His eyes stared. Boaz passed a hand before them. Nothing.

He touched Romrey's cheek. The flesh was hard and smooth, like stone.

Experimentally he nudged the rocklike body, then pushed it gently. Romrey toppled over, clanked dully to the floor of gold. Not a finger had shifted position.

Whatever had attacked Boaz, and been fought off by his ship, had attacked Romrey too. Boaz allowed his gaze to wander to three newly landed ships parked on the golden, shining landscape. The Hat Brothers stood staring at one another, or seeming to. They were utterly motionless.

He framed a question, staring at *The Sedulous Seeker.* "*The same,*" his ship answered, with an alacrity that showed it had already checked the yacht on its own initiative. Briefly it brought Boaz a cameo of Obsoc and Mace sitting together, also motionless.

Boaz came to a quick decision. He would take the stiffened bodies of Romrey, Obsoc and Mace aboard his ship and take off immediately, taking his chance on getting past the econosphere cruiser. In his haste he forgot, for the moment, his advance knowledge of his future words to the yacht robot. When he remembered them it was already too late to do anything, for the chess game began again. Once more Boaz was a manipulated piece. Once more he went through a dizzying sequence of impressions, too fast for him to be able to take in, in which colors, images and sounds flashed past.

But in what sense was he now being moved? He sensed that it was not just in time—perhaps not in time at all. After scant seconds all went black. He seemed to be hurtling down a dark tunnel. Then he was still, but in darkness, into which a yellow glow spread slowly.

The darkness fled, revealing that he stood in a dome-shaped chamber. Around him stood five or six of the ibis-headed creatures he had seen in the time-gem. They regarded him calmly, with beady eyes, their beaklike faces gleaming. They were, on average, a little shorter than a man, and their thin, smoothly muscled, olive-colored bodies appeared youthful, like the bodies of young girls—for, he noticed, they all lacked anything resembling male sex organs. The silver circlets around their waists, which comprised their only adornment, seemed, now that Boaz saw them more closely, to be in ceaseless motion, as if made of flowing quicksilver.

Despite the ordeal he had just been through, he did not feel particularly afraid of them. It was, however, an habituated response. He had encountered intelligent aliens several times before, and had come to learn that in general they were apt to offer him less threat than were strangers of his own species.

He did, on the other hand, feel awe. These were the beings who could manipulate time, to whom time was no more than an additional spatial dimension. They were, in other words, *four-dimensional beings*.

In comparison with ordinary creatures like Boaz, who crawled like worms from one moment to the next, that made them like gods. Were they, in fact, gods? And was not the ibis head, he recalled with an inward shudder, a symbol of the ancient god Thoth, said to have shown and explained the colonnader card pack to mankind long ago, before the technical age?

Once Boaz had asked Madrigo if there were gods.

Madrigo had answered: "There may be; it has not been settled. But if there are then they are transient and limited beings, as we are. More intelligent, more potent, with a consciousness whose relation to matter is perhaps somewhat different from ours, but that is all. One should not," he had added, "be afraid of any entity."

"They will not be immortal?" Boaz had asked.

"All beings are immortal," Madrigo had reminded him. "But like us, the gods must live and die."

The creature facing Boaz made a cryptic gesture, touching a finger to its flattened forehead. With the same flowing motion it turned, with an open hand indicating the curved wall behind it. Then the entire group turned, and filed out of the chamber to Boaz's left.

Boaz could not see the door they exited by. But in front of him, where there had been only blank wall a moment before, there was now an arched opening. A purple cloth screened the opening, waving slightly as if in a breeze. He stepped forward, touched the cloth—which wasn't there. There was just the feeling of something silky, like warm oil, touching his skin, and his hand went right through.

Boldly he walked through the screen, and stopped. He had entered a circular chamber like the first, but smaller. The walls and curved roof were of the same texture he had seen in the "city"—indeed, Boaz guessed that he was in fact back in the mysterious complex. This chamber, however, contained more by way of furniture, though he could only guess at the functions of the three or four cabinetlike objects standing on the floor.

On a raised, cushioned dais in the center of the room there sat, cross-legged, another of the ibis-headed aliens. At first sight it seemed indistinguishable from the others, but for some reason, as he looked at it, Boaz gained an impression of immense age and experience. Furthermore, as the beady, expressionless eyes stared back, he felt like a puddle into which some lofty entity was poking a finger, so that the ripples radiated out into every crevice of his being and were reflected back. There was absolutely no doubt of it: the creature was inspecting his mind.

"Come in, little Mudworm."

Again the hated nickname which, among so many other

factors, had helped make his life a misery in the Corsair warrens.

The voice was mature, full, human—and male. Hearing it was a trifle odd. One imagined it was spoken by the creature facing him, but the curved, tubelike beak was clearly unsuited to human speech, and the creature's head had not moved. The voice had emanated from empty air.

In spite of the irrational displeasure he felt at the reference to his early years, excitement mounted in Boaz. He had been given an interview with the inhabitants of Meirjain—with the time-gods, as he already thought of them! He could ask questions! He was close to learning what he needed to know!

"So you know our language," he began.

"Or you have been made to understand ours. What difference does it make? Come closer, Mudworm. Do not hover by the door."

"My name is Joachim Boaz," Boaz said sternly. But he obeyed, moving closer. The voice chuckled.

"Aggressive self-assertiveness, as ever with your species. Very well, Joachim Boaz, as you will."

"What shall I call you?" Boaz asked.

"I am myself. I need no name. Does that answer sound familiar to you?"

"No."

"It should. It is similar to an answer you once gave when asked the name of your ship."

"But we are not ships."

"Are *you* not? What are you without one?"

The creature clearly knew all about him. It was disconcerting to be so mentally naked. "I have questions," Boaz said. "But you already know what they are."

"You have questions. But discourse cannot be tacit. The mind must express itself."

Boaz almost smiled. It was a remark Madrigo himself might have made. The thought provoked Boaz into dipping his hand in a pocket and coming out with the colonnader pack. Expertly he flipped through the cards until coming to the Stellar Realm, which showed a naked woman pouring out water onto a landscape from two jugs. Behind her, an ibis was taking flight from an evergreen tree.

He held out the card before the Meirjain creature, pointing to the ibis. "First," he said excitedly, "did your species have contact with mine long ago? This picture is centuries old. Note the head of the bird. It symbolizes the god of all the sciences. Perhaps *you* taught *us* the beginnings. . . ."

His voice trailed off. The ibis-headed man leaned forward and inspected the card. "Yes, there is certainly a resemblance," the voice said. "But it means nothing. It is simply a matter of convergent evolution, arising from the manner of feeding. The general shape of my head is a commonly occurring one, as is the shape of yours. As for whether any of my colleagues visited your planets long ago, I have no idea. You have seen the big ships outside? They were mainly used for visiting foreign galaxies. But they have been laid up for a long time now."

Slowly Boaz put away the cards. He had forgotten all about Romrey and the others. The big, big question hung in his mind, and he was afraid to speak it.

He stood silent, dumb. The ibis-headed man's artificial voice spoke again, softly.

"Yes, I can help you, Joachim Boaz. But I wonder if you really want it, little Mudworm."

"You know I want it!" Boaz burst out. "It is all I want. You have conquered time! You can tell me how——"

He stopped, realizing the ridiculousness of his position, seeing how he had been reduced to helplessness. Why should these creatures help him? What interest had they in his mad scheme? And yet there was no way he could disguise his intention.

"Yes?" the voice said. "I can tell you how to alter time, you were about to say? There I can only disappoint you, Joachim Boaz. We cannot alter time, whether past, present or future. Time is inexorable."

"But I have *experienced* it!"

"Have you? Think. All I did was move your consciousness along your time-line. I can take you into your past, and a little way—only a little way—into your future. In the same way we can refract light through time, by means of the time-gems. Yes, the past and the future can be known. But as for altering anything—no. Does this sound like a paradox? It isn't really. I shall explain. As you have guessed, we are four-dimensional beings. But only in a sense. We have learned to do what I did for you—to move back and forth over our time-lines, though only to a limited degree into the future. No time transfer was involved in bringing you into this dwelling, incidentally. We merely put you through a displacement vortex, which is our normal way of traveling about the planet.

"You might think that the foreknowledge this gives us, by governing our actions, enables us to control and alter future time—but no. Everything that happens in my future is already a result of this foreknowledge. It cannot be changed. Our time-traveling ability is, itself, part of the predestined cosmic pattern."

Boaz stared at the ibis-headed man, a familiar burdensome feeling coming over him. "What is the good of such a faculty?" he asked.

"It adds an extra dimension to life, as you can appreciate. To return to the past is more efficient than memory, which is apt to be unreliable. Experience of the future is also more useful than mere prediction."

"You have some machinery for accomplishing this mental projection through time?"

"It is a mental discipline. There is no machinery for it."

"Would you teach it to me?"

"You could never learn it. Your brain is too different."

The right adplants, or else the right silicon bones, might rectify that, Boaz thought. But if what he had just been told was true, there would probably be little point in it. The time-gems in his pocket still seemed to offer him most hope. Whatever the ibis-headed man said, they were proof that there *was* a physical means of manipulating time.

"Then I thank you for your information. I would like to leave now."

"No, you cannot leave yet, Joachim Boaz. I have something more to tell you."

The ibis-headed man shifted slightly. His head turned, as if to glance at something on the wall, and for a moment Boaz saw the strange face in profile, looking exactly like the Egyptian bird in the colonnader card.

"Let me tell you what brought you here, what brought all the others here who landed in the last few hours. You see, I am very old. My species conquered the aging process long ago. My body will die only when accidental and un-repairable damage on the cellular level reaches a lethal ac-cumulation—which will happen eventually, of course. Now, beings that live a long time are liable to develop special hobbies, so as to while away the period of their ex-istence. My hobby is alien psychology. As our steerable planet wanders through the galaxy I make it my business to study the mental features of the various species we come across from time to time. This, let me add, is my own hobby. My friends and colleagues, some of whom you have just met, follow other interests. . . .

"But to come back to the point, Joachim Boaz. We have been in this star cluster for a while now, long enough for me to notice that your species possesses a certain psycho-logical peculiarity. This quirk could be summed up as *ob-sessiveness*. Never have I met a race with such a capacity for letting the mind become possessed with a desire or idea. It intrigues me considerably.

"So I decided to collect a few suitable specimens for study. Ordinary specimens were no good, I wanted those in whom this obsessive quirk is developed to a high degree. So I set up a *fly trap*. You know what a fly trap is? On your worlds you have troublesome insects, so you set a trap for them with something sweet and sticky. The sweetness attracts them, and the stickiness stops them from getting away. The flies cannot resist the sweetness, so they are bound to get caught. Do you see how I caught you all, little fly? You are all obsessed in one way or another— with greed, with desire for possession, with other, more in-teresting needs. . . . and Meirjain the Wanderer became the irresistible lure for you all! The ploy might be a con-venient way of ridding your society of its undesirable ele-ments—criminality, you see, is unusual among intelligent species. My own motive is not altruistic, however. I now have an adequate number of suitable specimens for future study."

"Then those people—are still alive?"

"Alive and fully conscious. But conscious in an unac-customed way. What else do you do with flies? You swat them. That is what I have done with the people who came here seeking their own ends. I stopped their consciousness at one moment of time. They live timelessly now, experiencing only that one moment, thinking their last thought, feeling their last feeling, seeing whatever happened in that instant. This mode of consciousness will be most strange for one of your kind. For me, of course, it is only a matter of convenience, a means of storage."

"Why are their bodies so stiff?"

"Their bodies persist, even though consciousness is locked in the past. They are rigid because the electrical forces between molecules have been rendered incapable of change."

"But it didn't work with me, did it?"

"No. Your ship saved you. It is a remarkable phenomenon. And you yourself are by far the most interesting of the specimens, Joachim Boaz. That is why I have brought you here. The others all have minds that, when we come down to it, are petty in their concerns. But you! You have set yourself to change time itself, to negate the whole universe if need be. Could any obsession be so grandiose? You have set yourself to fight Hercules, to pull the legs from under Atlas, to wrestle with Mother Kali, to joust with Jesus, to battle with Ialdabaoth. . . ."

Though he vaguely recognized the other names, only Atlas and Hercules were familiar to Boaz. They were ancient, cruder versions of the colonnader image of strength, or nature. "And you, I suppose, will tell me it is impossible," he said in a surly tone.

"Could it be possible? After all, a bacterium can slay a man. But to do that it must multiply itself indefinitely, and there is only one Joachim Boaz. Besides, a bacterium and a man are of almost the same size, when compared with the ratio between you and nature. And there is something else you must understand, Joachim Boaz. Even those gods I mentioned are powerless to change anything. They are powerless because they do not exist. All that exists is natural force, and in the last resort, the unconditioned consciousness that comes into its own between successive world manifestations. But even this super-personal consciousness can neither change anything nor even decide to change anything. It is only the real world made latent, and the real world is changeless. So you see, in your madness you are striving for the absolutely impossible.

"And yet I tell you, Joachim Boaz, that there is a way you can do it."

The narrow curved beak, so nearly motionless while they had been talking, dipped as if in thought. Boaz found that he could not speak, so great was the tension within him, and after a while the ibis-headed man continued: "Let me paint you a picture. You are walking down a street in one of your towns. The street forks both left and right. Both routes bring you to the ship ground where your ship is parked. Both routes take about the same time. Always at this moment, throughout all eternity, you have taken the left turn. *Can you now take the right turn instead?*"

"It is all that is needed," Boaz admitted. "I know this."

"But have you never tried to force yourself, in some such small action, to do *something new?*"

"Of course!" Boaz was familiar with this frustrating and futile exercise. A distressed frown crossed his face. "It is impossible to know! One can never remember what one's future action is supposed to be!"

"That is right. You cannot remember that you have lived before. You do not know what is supposed to happen. What you cannot remember, you cannot alter. Perhaps it would be easy to act differently if you could remember—who knows? But you cannot, so instead you look to science, to a mechanical device that can alter time for you. But you can never succeed that way, Joachim Boaz. No inanimate device can do it for you. *You must do it yourself.* You as you are cannot do it. The super-personal consciousness that keeps guard in the night of the world cannot do it. If it can be done at all, it can be done only by a new kind of consciousness—one that is personal, residing in a living creature, and yet *remembers.* Such a consciousness would be more intense than the abstract consciousness from which the world was originally made. It could act differently."

"This is all very well," Boaz rumbled, pondering as he listened, "but I don't have this new consciousness. And although I have received mental training, I have never heard of it before."

"Of course not. If it existed, the world would not repeat from phase to phase with such absolute precision. But you *can* have it, Joachim Boaz—if you are brave enough."

"I am brave enough," Boaz said immediately. "Tell me how."

"Are you? We shall see. Only a god could change the course of the universe, and in effect you are asking how to become a god, the first ever to exist, since there have been no gods up to now. Very well, I will tell you. To become a god you must bear the unbearable. What brought you to this extraordinary idea, in the first place? Transcendental pain! It opened the door to a new idea, a new vision. For a fact, it was an event never intended by nature. All these ages it has lain as a minute but imperceptible chink in nature's armor, a tiny flaw that conceivably could lead to her being overthrown. But the experience broke you, Joachim Boaz. You were unable to bear it; human consciousness is not strong enough.

"Nevertheless you must bear it. Only if an experience of that order can be faced, contained, endured without losing control, can the human mind transcend itself. And if it transcends itself, it transcends nature. I tell you, Joachim Boaz, this event would be unique, unprecedented in the history of the cosmos. You could be catapulted into a new order of being. *You would remember*, Joachim Boaz. *You would remember*, and remembering, you could alter what you remember. The world around you would become a machine under your control."

Boaz nodded, wondering what Madrigo would make of this.

But the news was not good enough for him. "You are telling me to wait, to be patient until the next manifestation of the world—and then to meet my misfortune in a different frame of mind. Your proposal is ludicrous."

"That is not what I propose, Joachim Boaz. There is no need to wait. With my help, you can do it now. I can return you to that horrendous event. *I can backtrack your consciousness through time, so that you live through it again.* But this time you must be prepared to conquer it.

"Well?" The ibis beak lifted challengingly. The small black eyes glittered.

When the shocking meaning of what the alien was offering came home to him, Boaz felt as though someone had punched him unexpectedly in the stomach. He flinched, he trembled, he was aghast.

"No. You can't expect—you couldn't expect me to agree to that—"

"You are afraid. It is natural. And yet you know that eventually it must come again, an unknown number of times, as the wheel turns. This is your chance to face it knowingly. Success is only a conceivable possibility, of course, not a guarantee. Perhaps you will triumph, perhaps you will sink into final insanity. But to become a god, you must have the daring of a god."

An irrational hatred of the ibis-headed man arose in Boaz, and with it an ungovernable panic. He was terrified that the alien might carry out the plan without permission. When he spoke, it was in a choking voice.

"Plainly there is a limit to your knowledge. You imagine that I—or anyone—could face *that*. It is not the way. There must be another way."

"There is no other way. You will accomplish nothing unless you conquer your fear. Fear rules you, little Mudworm. Fear drives you to everything. But it does not matter what I say to you. You will continue to convince yourself that a miracle can be worked by purely material means. I knew already that this would be the outcome. Think how often you have been given this one opportunity which you lack the courage to seize."

"How dare you say that to me." Boaz was sobbing. "You have not suffered as I have."

"The worm would become a god. But the worm has not the heart of a god. Go then, little Mudworm, and live out your useless life. I have finished studying you."

Boaz was enraged. He did not know, in that moment, whether he would attack the ibis-headed man or flee through the screen at his back. In any event, a black funnel formed suddenly in the air before him. He felt himself moving, traversing countless dizzying scenes as before.

Stillness again. He was standing on the plain of gold, which shone in the light of the yellow sun. The Hat Brothers stood near their ship, which was made tiny by the huge and gorgeous alien ships far off. A little farther away was Boaz's own ship, with *The Sedulous Seeker* behind it.

How much freedom would the ibis-headed man permit him? He shook off rage, shook off the sick feeling of having failed a crucial test. He shook off the resentment and contempt he felt for anyone, man or alien, who told him to endure what he was certain no being could endure.

He had the time-gems. He had an assurance, from his conversation with the ibis-headed man, that his quest was not *totally* hopeless, however qualified that statement might be. He could go forward.

He had to think how to leave Meirjain unmolested by the government cruiser. After only a moment's deliberation he lifted Romrey's statuelike body onto the sledge and set off for *The Sedulous Seeker*.

He could not resist slowing down as he passed the Hat Brothers. They were staring sightlessly at one another. As the time-swat jointly hit them, it must have been the last thing they did. That mutual look was now made timeless.

At the yacht Obsoc's robots greeted him worriedly with concerned news of Obsoc and Mace, neither of whom, it seemed, could be roused. Boaz directed the sledge into the lounge, where he briefly inspected the two.

He spoke to one of the yacht robots. "Take off and enter circumpolar orbit, achieving stable velocity over the magnetic north pole. Meanwhile broadcast a surrender message to the government cruiser. With luck they will intercept you rather than shoot you down, and you can gain medical assistance for your master and his friends."

The robot inclined its head in understanding. Boaz turned to go, then paused. Already he had saved Mace from self-destruction. By his ethic, he had an obligation to her.

He did not think the time-stop would prove permanent or incurable once they were away from Meirjain. But her future with Obsoc would probably land her in the same psychological state as before.

"Move the girl onto my sledge," he ordered the robots. He left the yacht with her, and minutes later was aboard his own ship. He watched *The Sedulous Seeker* lift off. When he gauged that the econosphere cruiser would be moving to intercept it, he ordered his own ship up.

In the opposite direction, he hurtled in a low, flat trajectory. Over the south magnetic pole he piled on power and shot away from the planet, using it to screen his ship. Soon he was through the *c* barrier and safe.

Only then did he realize he had forgotten something. He should have taken Romrey's time-gems from his belt pouch. Romrey, if he did come out of time-stop, was going to be in deep trouble over those gems.

Chapter

SIX

The matter of the meeting was so secret that all but three of those present would be subjected to memory elision before leaving the building. The privileged three had ordered the meeting. Two were econospheric councillors. The third, a man with steady blue eyes and an impassive gaze, was the heavily adplanted Director of the Department of Scientific Affairs. All three were members of the Cabal, the inner and semi-secret society by means of which the econospheric government buffered and protected its business.

Seated triumvirate fashion on the traditional raised dais, they loomed like judges over the dozen or more advisers squatting on cushions arranged in a horseshoe on the floor. These, too, were nearly all government employees—scientists, philosophers, policemen. The exception was a quiet individual who had been brought all the way from the famed colonnader planet of Aurelius. To him the trio paid a more discernible, if grudging, respect.

Not until they had settled themselves were the advisers informed that they were to discuss infringements of Article 70898/1/5: *Regulations Concerning the Measurement of Time.* It was in these regulations, so as not to draw undue attention to it, that the prohibition on time research was buried. The first stage of the meeting, officially called "Presentation of the Problem," was nearly over. The gathering was watching a recording on a police interrogation, and on the holocast a lean-faced man, still

113

younger rather than middle-aged, swayed drunkenly in the straps of the chair that held him. His mind was being played back with no less trouble than a voice tape.

Gare Romrey was that man, recovered from time-stop, charged with possession of prohibited artifacts, all legal rights waived in the interests of state security. "The man's crazy," he was mumbling. "The craziest alec I ever came across. By the cards, I was glad to get away from him. . . ."

The picture faded as Romrey slumped. The whole story had been drained from him.

Into the silence that followed, Cere Chai Hebron, the Scientific Director, spoke. "From the information obtained from this man, from the other criminal Radalce Obsoc whose confession you have also seen, and from the robots who accompanied the latter, a probability analysis has been made of the period the fugitive Joachim Boaz spent upon the wandering planet. It is estimated with a weighted probability of around sixty-eight percent that the fugitive gained some information concerning time control that could not be perceived by his companion Romrey— remember Romrey's puzzlement that Boaz decided to leave the alien complex so abruptly, at a point where it might seem the search was most in prospect of greater success. Added to this, possession of the time-refractive gems itself opens up the likelihood of illegal experimentation, with a weighted probability of nearly ninety-seven percent that prohibited data will be obtained—data, incidentally, not available to the authorities themselves, since previously all circulating time-gems had been confiscated and placed under interdict.

"It might be asked why an expedition of foray is not sent to Meirjain to ascertain the validity of these conclusions. The fact is that although less than a standard year has passed since the events in question took place, the planet has already disappeared back into the Brilliancy Cluster and has proved unlocatable.

"I now ask Citizen Orskov, Dean of Moss Corporated Laboratories, to speak."

The designated academic, grey-haired, with a mild manner and a slight nervous affliction that caused him to jerk his head a little as he spoke, did not rise. "A few months

ago we were asked by the Department to make a fresh examination of the Mirror Theorem," he began. "For the
benefit of those who may not be acquainted with it, the
Mirror Theorem describes the motions of point masses
through eternity. Put briefly, it states that if an intersection
is made at any arbitrary moment in time, the world-lines
produced by the future configurations of the totality of
point masses in the universe will be an identical reflection
of the past configurations. In less technical language, the
theorem proves, given a sufficiently long span of time, the
periodic recurrence of the universe.

"Philosophically speaking there has always been a miss-
ing piece in this theorem. It deals with a closed system. Its
prediction that the future will exactly repeat the past arises
from the mechanical determinism inherent in the movements of masses. For a loose illustration of this principle,
we can refer to its earliest historical exposition by the pre-
scientific philosopher Lucretius. Working purely with in-
ductive, observational methods, Lucretius produced an
account of nature that in many respects was remarkably
correct. He pictured the universe as consisting of particles
or atoms falling through an endless void. As they fell the
particles collided, tangled with and parted from one another, and the impermanent configurations that resulted
comprised the worlds and their contents. Since the particles must eternally continue to fall, and since the number
of possible configurations is limited, it follows that the
same configurations, that is, the same worlds, beings and
events, must recur again and again.

"For Lucretius's perpetual falling we can substitute its
modern equivalent, the law of conservation of mass and
energy which, in general terms, represents the endless momentum inherent in matter. What the Mirror Theorem
lacks, however, is any term showing that the theorem is
rigorous. The theorem is valid not of necessity, but simply
because what it describes *is* a closed sytem. It has yet to
be shown what would happen were an extraneous factor,
by some unimaginable means, to be inserted into this system. What could be extraneous to the universe, you may
ask? That is why this feature of the Mirror Theorem has
never been taken seriously, and why to all intents and purposes the theorem has been regarded as rigorous.

"Nevertheless, it is thought that the configurations exhibited by our universe in its lifetime do *not* exhaust all *possible* configurations, and therefore alternative universes are at least conceivable."

With that, the academic sat silent, nodding to himself and smiling.

"Well, and what did your examination yield?" Director Hebron prodded impatiently.

"Hm? Oh yes. So sorry. No change. We could not prove the rigorousness of the Mirror Theorem. The mutability of time remains theoretically possible."

One of the econospheric councillors nodded gravely, and took up the theme. "Extraordinary though it may seem, this is the possibility we must seriously consider. Ever since the non-rigorousness of the Mirror Theorem was discovered, we have had to take account of the fact that there *might*, however low the order of probability, be a means whereby the unfolding progression of events could be turned aside. We know what this means, do we not? It means that the magnificent stability which the econosphere enjoys, and which is guaranteed eternal by cosmic recurrence, could be nullified. The next manifestation of the world could be one in which the econosphere does not exist, in which none of us exists. The time regulations are there to guard against this remote possibility."

What grotesque grandiosity, thought Madrigo as he listened to the discussion. It was a case of political ideology arrogating cosmic proportions to itself—a peculiarly gross overestimate of the importance of mankind.

The econosphere, slowly but steadily falling into decay, already owing its grandeur to the past rather than to present vigor, still retained its traditional creed of permanence and stability. From colonnader philosophy it had borrowed the idea of the eternal city and applied it, not to the sidereal realm of the galaxies, which was its proper meaning, but to its own existence. Faced with the knowledge that it must eventually collapse and disappear, it found its salvation in the greater and absolute permanence of cosmic recurrence. The econosphere would never perish, because ultimately nothing ever did.

Now its leaders had conceived a paranoiac suspicion that the course of nature, even on this the vastest of scales, could be interfered with. It reminded Madrigo of psycho-pathological religions of the past, which had gone so far as to put individuals on trial for "sabotage against God."

A question was being raised by the scientists on the floor. Nothing, they pointed out, lay outside nature. How, therefore, could the human mind find the fresh impulse that could lead it to alter time, even if it were technically feasible? Did that not contradict the principle of predetermination, which was supposed to govern human actions as well as everything else?

"The determinacy of nature has never been absolutely established, either," the Dean of Moss Corporated Laboratories responded diffidently. "If temporal mutability is possible, then it shows that nature, to some degree, perhaps hidden until now, is potentially indeterminate."

"Nevertheless, we would be faced with the incredible fact that this individual, this shipkeeper Joachim Boaz, must already have come in possession of some mental quality that is uniquely new, if he is to have any prospect of success. The indeterminacy of nature must already have shown itself."

This remark came, in a more forthright manner, from a man wearing the collar of the Research Tabulation Branch of the Department of Scientific Affairs. He apparently had the ear of Director Hebron, for the latter nodded approvingly. "As you say, there is something interesting here. We know, of course, how the fugitive came to conceive his ambition. It arose from his very unusual experience, an accidental combination of silicon bone functions and the pain-feeling function of the sensorium. It must be assumed that it is this that has introduced an indeterminate note into nature, if indeed any exists. . . ." Abruptly he turned to a burly, big-bellied figure in grey uniform who previously had not spoken. "How much pain can one experience? Is it known?"

The person he addressed was Chief of the Rectification Branch of the Department of Police, the arm of the police force charged more than any other with the impossible task of enforcing the econosphere's political laws. For a moment the police chief looked embarrassed; then he recovered himself and his lip curled in a half-smile of ill-veiled relish.

"This question has received some investigation, of course," he said in an impressively heavy baritone. "The problem has always been to maintain the subject's consciousness while continuing to increment pain levels. Consequently the absolute limit of pain has never been reached by us, surprising though that might seem. The silicon bone gimmick sounds like a good one. I'll see that it's followed up."

"Please do not do so," Hebron said politely but firmly. "At least not for the present, until we can clear this whole matter up. We do not want any more Joachim Boazes wandering around."

Throughout the conference Hebron had been glancing at Madrigo, as if expecting him to take part in the exchanges. Madrigo rose to his feet now, in defiance of established protocol which required those on the floor to remain seated.

"Allow me to introduce myself," he said, gathering in the folds of his cyclas. "I know more than any of you about this man you are discussing. I was his mentor in Aurelius."

He paused, while his gaze traveled coolly over the gathering. "Firstly, let me say that any properly trained colonnader like myself will regard your talk regarding alterations to nature as simple foolishness. It is what one can expect from pure scientists. They become hypnotized by their ability to calculate, they allow themselves to become lost in the byways of a logical maze, and so they lose their sense of proportion. They forget, too, that all their science is founded on deeper philosophical ideas. And from the standpoint of genuine philosophy, I can tell you categorically that there can be no alteration to the predestination of time. Whatever happens, the next universe will be an exact reproduction of this one.

"As for Joachim Boaz, I am sorry to say that his truly harrowing experience has broken his mind, so that he is now even beyond my help. I am certain that he is quite insane, with no vestige of ataraxy. To conjoin in his delusions is undignified in a department of government."

An initial silence followed Madrigo's words. Then a babble of argument began. One of the econospheric ministers raised his hand, at which the noise stopped.

He conferred briefly with his two colleagues, in tones which the others could not decipher. Then he turned back to face the gathering.

"The sense of the meeting is that a situation exists where a derangement of the structure of time could be possible," he said coldly, "and that this constitutes a threat to the econosphere. We order that the individual Joachim Boaz be found and destroyed. The colonnader"—he cast an unfriendly glance at Madrigo—"is to be held until that is done, for any further assistance he can render."

Hearing of his pending detention, Madrigo understood that its main purpose was to prevent him from getting a warning to Boaz—even though, on the face of it, memory elision would render it unnecessary. Econosphere officials had a sometimes exaggerated respect for the mental abilities of colonnaders.

He noted, as the meeting broke up, that the police chief's eyes gleamed with the prospect of the hunt. Even though he, too, after the next few minutes, would not know why the man he hunted was a danger to society.

Chapter

SEVEN

"This is a nice one," said Mace.

Boaz had left his colonnader cards on the table. Mace had been sorting idly through them, and now was inspecting Major Arcanum number twenty. It was the card called Unveiling. Specifically, the veil that in the card called the Priestess had hung between the pillars *Joachim* and *Boaz* had now been drawn aside and was draped along one edge of the card. The scene it revealed was unworldly. A mythical semi-human figure, with richly pinioned wings half unfolded to extend rakishly along its back, hovered in a horizontal posture over an indistinct landscape. The "angel," as the figure was called, held to its lips a long, slender trumpet that itself seemed to float endlessly over this same landscape, so elongated was it. The trumpet evidently gave voice to a powerful blast, of a force so great that the group of people who threw up their hands in its path was being dispersed.

Dissolution was the meaning of the card: it depicted, in parabolical language, the time when the universe would collapse into fire and come to an end. The pillars of existence would fall into one another, and the latent, unmanifest eons would begin.

The slight movement of the ship stopped. It had completed its short journey across the ship ground and had entered an underground parking shed. Boaz had taken this precaution to try to reduce the possibility of early discovery by the authorities.

From his armchair, he looked across the table at Mace. They had been together for nearly a year now, hiding in space or on fringe worlds to evade the police hunt which he was sure would be taking place. She had come out of time-stop when they were exactly ten light-hours from Meirjain, and she had told him, when she was able to speak, what it was like to be trapped in one moment in time: an experience which, perhaps, could only be comprehended, and that only partially, by a bone man or woman who had experienced the elongated time sense of altered chronaxy. It had clearly had an effect on her, giving her eyes a drugged, haunted look which faded only after some days.

He should have parted company with her, but he had not. He sensed that she had not yet shaken off the wish to commit suicide, and his colonnader obligations still told on him. He had embarked on a course of mental therapy, of the kind that had so deftly been practiced on him when he was a boy in Theta, and of whose methods his subsequent training had given him some knowledge.

It was odd, he admitted, that a man bent on total self-obliteration should, in passing, bother to mend the self-feeling of someone else. Mace, of course, had no idea that any form of process was being practiced on her. Colonnader techniques were not that formal. All she knew was that she had close discussions with Boaz, and that somehow her attitude toward herself gradually changed.

They had come to know one another well in the past year. Boaz, his tongue loosened perhaps by his earlier disclosure to Gare Romrey, as well as by the confidentiality of the therapist-patient relationship, had even confessed the nature of his mission to Mace.

She had listened with fascination, and none of the criticism or uncomprehending blame he could have expected from most. "But what does your mentor say to this?" she asked eventually.

"Madrigo?" Boaz made a wry face. "He thinks I have fallen victim to cachexia. He does not admit the possibility of what I am trying to do."

"Cachexia?"

"Mental disturbance. An ill-conditioned state of mind.

When colonnaders use the term, it betokens a particularly serious kind of mental illness."

"Do *you* think you could have it?"

"Of course I have it. The mistake is in thinking it is based on delusion. True, all other cases of cachexia *are* based on delusion. But in me it is based on reality. A reality deeper than any that underpins sanity. Not even Madrigo understands that."

He sighed, the conversation coming briefly to his memory, and rose. "It is time for me to find my friends, Mace. You may go into the city if you wish. Or remain here. You have your own key."

She nodded, and carried on sorting through the cards. Boaz hesitated; he would have liked to ask her for them, preferring to have them with him always, but decided it would be impolite. He left the ship, passed up the flow-elevator to the surface, and ventured cautiously onto the street.

He had wondered if he could have handled events better on Meirjain, but could see no ethical way in which he could have prevented his identity from becoming known to the authorities. Since then he was almost certainly a fugitive (although he had heard no official posting of his name) and the necessity of maintaining close proximity to his ship was proving a decided disadvantage. It was, in fact, the main reason why he had delayed events by nearly a year while he skulked on the edge of the econosphere, only now reckoning it relatively safe to come to Kathundra, a member of the Central Clique of worlds, a seat of government, though only one of several, a center of science and learning, and home of vices more sophisticated and depraved than raw boundary planets had yet imagined.

Mace, he imagined, would have a good time here. At other ports of call he had sometimes had occasion in passing to glance at her erotic adventures during his voyeuristic surveys.

She had once, with some eagerness, offered herself to him, but he had been obliged to decline. When he shut down his bone functions long ago, he had relinquished all sexual feeling with them.

He took a deep breath. At last he was on the planet Kathundra, in the city of Kathundra (on all Clique worlds the capital bore the same name as the planet). Here, within the ten miles of freedom his ship allowed him, was the man who all these years had been waiting for him.

He strolled for a while through the glittering walkways, interrogating his ship with orders to ascertain whether he was under observation. Because his shabby modsuit identified him as an outworld visitor, he was constantly beset by commercial adflashes and come-ons, as well as accosted by various individuals offering services likely to be sought by the tourist, and all of which he rudely refused. Finally satisfied that he had done all he could, he entered a travel agency. Kathundra boasted a modern transport system working on the instantaneous acceleration principle—an adaptation of star drive—and all he had to do was wait his turn at a line of stage chambers, dial a number and step inside. The door slid shut behind him, sealing the ceramic-lined cubicle with a hiss. He was seized in a complex field of uni-directional electrostatic forces which separated ever so slightly the positive and negative charges of every atom in his body. Other, more powerful uni-directional fields were added, acting on those charges and accelerating Boaz down a ceramic-lined tunnel. He passed through perhaps thirty switching points in the process of being routed to his destination, his velocity retarded or accelerated in each case so as to slot him in with millions of others passing through those same points. Boaz was not aware of what was happening, of course. The entire process, involving a roundabout journey of perhaps ten miles, took place in the standard interval of one-twentieth of a second. All he was conscious of was that a light came on and the cubicle number on the wall suddenly changed. He stepped out into the house of Aban Ebarak.

For a moment Boaz felt slightly dizzy, a consequence of the generally excellent transport system unique to him. While he was in the acceleration fields his ship's beams, though they were able to track him, were vitiated in their integrative functions. If he were trapped in the system for, say, a matter of minutes, he would probably die.

He stood in a small vestibule. To one side a broad window (which Boaz knew to be genuine, not a display) revealed that the scientist Ebarak's house was half a mile up a tower block and gave a breathtaking view of the jungle of shafts which was Kathundra. Ebarak himself was not in evidence, though Boaz had received the acceptance signal before stepping into the stage chamber. The scientist had, in fact, been expecting him for days.

Pausing to recover from the journey, he moved to a door and opened it, disclosing a neat study. Ebarak was within, poring over a reading screen. He looked up at the intrusion, a smallish, tidy man, with a pale face, chiseled nose, and mild blue eyes, which, when they were directed at anything or anyone, seemed to turn flint-hard.

"Ah, hello, Joachim. Sorry I wasn't on hand to greet you. I was just reading up on some material here. The memory gets a bit rusty, you know." Ebarak was one of many scientists who did not trust adplants too far, believing them to make the intellect lazy. He did not have a single memory adplant and only a standard type of adplanted calculator. The book he was reading on the screen, Boaz saw, was one on the econosphere's index of prohibited texts: Whitlaw's *Cases of Relativistic Event Reversal*. It dealt with the way in which time order could seemingly be reversed in small, insignificant ways as a result of the relativity laws.

The scientist killed the screen as he stood up. His mouth firmed. "Have you got them with you?"

"I have." Boaz took a pouch from a pocket of his modsuit. He handed it to Ebarak, who loosened the cord at the neck and poured out a number of gems onto the palm of his hand.

"They look so ordinary, don't they?" he murmured.

Laying the pouch on his desk, he picked up a gem between thumb and finger and brought it close to his eye, peering intently. After a moment in which he rolled the gem to tilt facet after facet, Ebarak saw a tiny scene. He saw himself, in his laboratory, fitting something gem-sized into an instrument with a long, shiny barrel.

He smiled. He was, he realized, looking a few minutes into his own future.

It was not the first time he had seen such gems. Briefly he had begun to investigate two specimens brought back from the first landings on Meirjain, before the Scientific

Ministry for which he then worked had closed down all such work in panic and impounded the jewels. He believed they had been destroyed.

"Thank you," he said with feeling. "Thank you."

"When shall I see you again?"

"Call me in a few days. Better leave now. I want to get down to work."

"Yes, of course." Shyly, hesitantly, Boaz turned to go. He would have liked to stay, to watch or assist his co-conspirator, But he knew that Ebarak did not want him there, and besides, the longer he stayed the more he increased the danger to the scientist.

He dialed the same travel agency he had come by and emerged, only slightly unsteady, back onto the walkway. For some time he drifted with the throng as before. Then he entered an eating house, sat and watched the passersby through the transparent frontage. As he knew from his previous visit, when he had sought and eventually made the acquaintance of Aban Ebarak, Kathundra was a place of affected mannerisms. People who met on the street greeted one another with exaggerated gestures and flourishes. Which, he supposed, made the offhanded casualness of Ebarak a distinctive mark of individuality.

After a while he returned to his ship. Mace was not there. He sat in his armchair, relaxed, and fell into a semi-doze. Without any prompting on his part, the ship began to send out its spy-beams, bringing him the habitual montage of scenes from the surrounding city.

He paid them only a fraction of his attention; he was like a man who kept the video switched on all the time. He showed a little more interest when the beam brought him a picture of Mace. It was hardly a coincidence, especially in a city of such size. Boaz had realized that the ship showed him Mace much more often than chance would account for. It was, he reasoned, obeying his subconscious wish to keep watch over her.

Usually he did not linger over her escapades, but this time some unformed impulse made him hold the image steady. Mace was in a private room with two others, a man and a woman. The woman was voluptuous like Mace, with heavy breasts and hips: the nymphgirl fashion was long out of date here on Kathundra. All three were

naked, except that the man and woman wore gas masks.
And they were spraying some kind of pearly mist over
Mace from nozzles they held in their hands. The mist bil-
lowed over her skin and seemed to be absorbed by it. It
drifted in her mouth and nostrils. As all this happened, her
face took on a look of extraordinary, ever-increasing ecstasy.

Boaz knew that the mist was a sex-enhancing drug. He
knew, too, from the look on Mace's face, that she had
switched on several of her bone functions.

The man and woman put aside the nozzles, ripped off
their gas masks, and fell together on Mace. In moments all
three were squirming and rocking together. Boaz, seeing
the incredible intensity of the pleasure Mace was experiencing, was struck by a totally new thought which brought
him instantly to wakefulness.

Could there be, to the horrendous *negative* experience
that had ruined his life, a *positive* one of equal intensity?
Was it possible to know pleasure, or happiness, in the
same degree in which he had known pain and misery?

Could *that* be his salvation? Could there be a canceling
of effects?

Gradually he faded out Mace's continuing transports of
delight. He ordered the spy-beam withdrawn from the city
and then sat alone in the darkness. It seemed a wonder to
him that he had never considered this before. After all,
equilibrium was one of the basic principles of the colonnader card pack. . . .

But no. The idea was fanciful, absurd. It seemed that
his long cohabitation with the girl was causing his mind to
wander.

He began thinking about the time-gems, and to wonder
instead if Aban Ebarak would make any progress.

Chapter

EIGHT

Two local days later Aban Ebarak received another visit, this time entirely unannounced.

But it was not without forewarning. He had rigged up a simple apparatus to project the images flashing so unpredictably from the time-gems onto a screen (though he had not, yet, worked out a way to capture a gem's output on all facets simultaneously). On the screen, the door of the laboratory opened and a tall slender figure, wearing a hooded street cloak clasped at the throat, entered. Ebarak was able to study the face for several seconds before the image faded.

By resuming the investigation so rudely interrupted years before, he had been able to calibrate the angle through which light was refracted on entering a gem. The scene he was witnessing registered a time bracket of five minutes either way of the present. Since it had not happened yet, it would happen shortly.

Patiently he waited, until a small sound came from the other side of the door.

"Come in, Cere," he called without turning his head.

The door opened and in walked Cere Chai Hebron, Director of the Department of Scientific Affairs, and econospheric Cabal member.

"How did you recognize me?" Hebron said in genuine surprise. He undid his cloak's throat-clasp, threw back the hood and pulled a flat, flesh-colored device from the side of his neck. Immediately his face began to change its appearance, no longer pulled into a false shape by the device's neurological control over his facial muscles. The real face that now showed was pale and finely chiseled, like Ebarak's, but unlike his it had a sultriness about the mouth, a hint of passion about the eyes, when Hebron listened or spoke intently.

"The eyes, Cere," Ebarak said. "You forgot to disguise the eyes. That gadget couldn't fool me." He was amused. A survey had once revealed that thirty-eight percent of scientific workers—a far higher percentage than chance could account for—had eyes of the same cool blue hue. There was still argument over what the finding meant.

Hebron sighed. It was a habit of people of his class to disguise themselves when moving alone in public. In this case he had an additional reason for doing so. He was putting himself at risk by being here at all.

"There's something else," Ebarak said. "You probably imagine I saw you come into the vestibule through a monitor. I didn't. I watched you enter this laboratory—in advance."

He spun a wheel, backtracking the recorder and running the scene again for Hebron's benefit.

"Time-gem?" Hebron asked, staring at the few seconds of action in fascination.

"Yes. You already know I have them, of course. That's what brings you here." He paused. "It would make a good warning system, if it could be made reliable."

"But productive of paradoxes?" Hebron suggested as the scene faded.

"Oh, I don't think so. Paradoxes don't exist in the real world." Ebarak turned away from the screen, switched off the apparatus and swiveled to face Hebron. "I would have gotten word to you that I have the gems. You know that, don't you?"

"Do I?" said Hebron acidly. Feeling the heat of the laboratory, he removed his cloak. Draping it over one arm, he stared down at Ebarak in schoolmasterly fashion. "You should have let me know *immediately*. This matter has been given top priority. It is only a matter of time before Orm's bloodhounds track you down, and this Joachim Boaz, too. I shall protect you for as long as I can, but it would be easier if you had confided in me."

"Orm?"

"He's now chief of the Rectification Branch. And he's a brute, I promise you."

"How did you find out I have the gems?"

"My own people have been watching you. You met Boaz once, years ago. It seemed possible he would seek your help."

Ebarak raised his eyebrows. "You knew of my acquaintance with Boaz?"

"You told me, at the time."

"Did I?" said Ebarak vaguely. His eyes glazed in a vain effort at recollection. This time it was Hebron's turn to smile, partly with exasperation. Scorning memory adplants, Ebarak was prone to these blank spots in his knowledge of past details.

"How many gems did Boaz give you?" Hebron asked.

"Twelve. But I believe he may have more."

"Let me see one."

A trifle reluctantly, Ebarak went to a safe, bent to its audio plate where he quietly hummed a series of tones, and opened the thick metal door. He took out the pouch Boaz had given him, carefully extracted a gem, and handed it to Hebron.

The Director lifted the gem to the light, peering into its depths. He rolled it, chuckling.

"It's genuine! And so clear! This is like old times, Aban! This time let's try to ensure that they stay in our possession."

He handed back the gem. "But we must get properly organized. I hope you didn't have thoughts of working on your own? You'll get nowhere that way. What's needed is teamwork." He stroked his jaw thoughtfully. "Also your facilities here are too limited—quite apart from what will happen if *Orm* learns of your past relationship with Boaz."

Ebarak swiveled his chair so that he was in profile to the Director and gazed into the distance, as though not wanting to hear what Hebron had said. Hebron leaned back against a workbench, supporting himself with his hands, and scrutinized his old friend. "I see you are displeased."

"It's just that I'm not convinced people with philosophi-

cal commitments can produce good scientific work,"
Ebarak said in a neutral tone.

Hebron was not offended. "The pure scientist, as ever!
Excellent. It is why we value you."

"Also I do not share this aim of yours."

"Do you not? Yet you seem willing to work toward its
accomplishment. . . . Yes, I know, it is disinterested
research where you are concerned. The pure search for
knowledge. And yet the great transformation might be
achieved. Temporal mutation might become possible.
Think what you will have unleased on the world! Reckless-
ness of that order, simply in the quest for knowledge, bor-
ders on a philosophical commitment all of its own."

"Except that these gems may not lead to what you
want. I have no reason to think they do."

"And have you communicated that belief to Boaz? After all, *his* aim is the same as mine."

"He is a man obsessed, in a way that even you are not.
He forms his own opinions."

"And you exploit that obsession to get what *you* want.
You see, we all use each other. In this case you have no
choice but to work with my team. You need me to ward
off Orm—if I can. Otherwise I do not think you will live
long enough to contemplate, in your intellectual purity, the
new knowledge of time you may glean from these gems."

Ebarak turned his head sharply toward the Director.
"Do *you* never contemplate the risks you are taking? You
are a member of the Cabal, yet you are committing what
amounts to state treason. I do not think *you* will suffer a
simple death, when you are found out. They will make a
terrible example of you."

"I *will* enjoy a simple death," Hebron said quietly. "It is
already arranged. I assure you I am not oblivious to the
risk. As for why I take it, your friend Joachim Boaz understands it even if you do not. *He* believes it is possible to
lift the dead hand of predestination. Do you never feel it
pressing down on your every deed, Aban? Does the impos-
sibility of original action never depress you?"

"No, because what you are saying is philosophy, in
other words, it is imagination."

"It is fact. What a stubborn refusal to appreciate reality!"

"Your lack of caution amazes me, nevertheless," Ebarak persisted mildly. "Being such a prominent figure, you are skimming very close to the event horizon." He was using a contemporary figure of speech that, in an earlier age, might have emerged as "skating on thin ice."

"Oh, but I am a powerful man, Aban. You must rely on obscurity for your protection, but I can employ econo- sphere resources to avoid discovery. Besides, it is now a matter of urgency. There is something I might as well tell you. You said to me once that even if a way to alter pre- destination could be found, the changes that could be made would be trivial. I have put some of the best brains in the econosphere to work on just that point, and what they say is this: a small change in *this* universe will effect a total change in the next one. Changes wrought in the current manifestation may well be trivial, as you predict—perhaps even imperceptible. But it is during the latent period, not the material one, that the consequences of those changes work themselves through. Here is an analogy: immerse alum crystals in water, heat it and the crystals will dissolve and disappear. Cool the solution again, and the crystals will reappear *in the same formation as before*. But what if the solution is stirred while hot? Then the case is not the same. The crystals will arrange themselves differently on their next materialization."

Ebarak listened closely while Hebron went on: "So you see, Aban, there is a race on. Whoever succeeds in this thing will have the key to unimaginable power, if it can be controlled. I sense that it *will* succeed; the process is under way. But by whom will it be accomplished? If your work does not produce results then Joachim Boaz, for instance, will go elsewhere, and perhaps, eventually, he will succeed. So if we die, still not masters of our fates, we cannot be sure what will become of us in our next resurrection, and perhaps as individuals we will cease to exist at all, forever.

"Tell me," he said after a long pause, "did Boaz have a woman with him?"

"He had no one with him."

"There is evidence that he had a woman with him when he fled Meirjain. Is he residing in the city?"

"I believe so."

"He has a deficiency, a physical dependence on his

spaceship. He is unable to stray far from it . . . his ship may even be hidden somewhere near the ship ground. I will investigate. . . ."

He dropped his eyes and fell silent. Ebarak said nothing. Hebron, he knew, was thinking that the woman he had mentioned would be a good source of information about Boaz. But he did not want to feel curious about what such a line of inquiry entailed.

Idly he switched on the projector again. A picture formed on the screen, snatched from out of near-time. With relief he saw a cloaked and hooded Hebron, a few minutes in the future, depart from his laboratory.

Exuding an odor of sweat laden with pheromonic musk, Eystrach Orm moved down the line of young men bent over their monitor desks. As he passed, each junior policeman felt a tremor of terror mingled with lust.

Everyone who worked in that department had to come to terms with Orm's tastes. He liked young men, but he liked them to be heterosexual, and to overpower their natural repugnance for his advances. Dismay, horror and unwilling but irresistible attraction were for him an indispensible sexual recipe. To this end he used not only his rank, not only his impressive physical presence, but also crudely chemical means. The scent he wore contained concentrated organic compounds that overcame almost any male's resistance.

"Sir."

"Yes?" Orm strode to a monitor who had raised his arm. He bent to the screen, placing his hands on the youth's shoulders and squeezing slightly as he brought his head close to his.

"Look, sir." The policeman was twisting slide-dials, trying to sort the signal he had traced from the rest of the city's traffic and bring it up on the screen.

Orm frowned at the flickering, fading pattern in pastel colors that was brought to the screen. "It looks like noise. Probably just reflection."

This section prided itself on being able to intercept any beamed signal in the city. "That's what I thought it was, sir—a double reflection, it's so faint. The general traffic completely hides it normally. But—"

"Yes?" Orm's hand was fondling his subordinate's neck.

"It has a constant level, sir. It must be a deliberate output."

"But it's too low. It isn't a useful signal."

"No sir. But I can't understand its multiplexing either."

"Keep on it. Let me know if you need a filter-booster."

"Yes sir."

Orm's hand dropped from the policeman's neck. He prowled away, left the monitor room and came to where the outworld reports were being sifted. "Well?"

Seated at a datagrator was an officer wearing silver braid. His eyes looked dazed as he rapidly absorbed the results that were being fed to his adplant through a silver nerve in his thumb. At the same time a broad-angle holdisplay was before him, though Orm couldn't see it from where he stood.

The officer came out of his near-trance. "It's shaping up, sir. Two positive placings, a significant curve of probables over the year. It looks as if he's moving in this direction."

"Eh? The cheeky bastard." Orm studied a dataplate the officer handed him. The difficulty in these cases sprang from the total lack of migration or trade controls on nearly every planet of the econosphere. A man could land and take off without anybody bothering him, and could even pay his shipground dues without leaving a record of his identity. Despite that, detective work was straightforward. One simply collected, through a far-flung plethora of spies, informers and data machines, a billion or more small facts which were analyzed statistically. It always brought results, given enough time. Amazingly trivial objects could be tracked, such as items of cargo.

"Do you think he could actually be *here*?" Orm asked wonderingly. "In Kathundra?" It seemed irresponsibly reckless—unless the desperate shipkeeper had a reason good enough to risk it.

He thought of the mysterious minimum-power signals the monitor had picked up. There could be a connection with the physical reliance the ex-colonnader was supposed to have on his converted cargo ship. The prisoner Romrey had spoken of its unusual communication system.

If Boaz was already in Kathundra, then Orm's quarry was trapped.

"We might snuff out this one sooner than we thought," he said with a purr of pleasure. He smiled, feeling a touch of excitement, the excitement of a chase nearing its end. Excitement caused him to sweat more, and as his evaporating perspiration cast extra pheromonic volatiles into the air, his sexual presence became all the stronger.

Moving with the burly grace of a puma, he padded back to the monitor room.

Chapter

NINE

"Look."

Captain Joachim Boaz awoke.

He was alone in the ship. Mace had not been there for over three days, but that was no surprise. Her absences were becoming longer.

He did not answer. But he felt, impinging on his brain, one end of a very long stick. That stick was a spy-beam that extended seven miles or more.

The other end of the beam showed him Mace. At first he wondered why the ship had roused him just to show him one more of her erotic episodes. It was a good part of a minute before he realized that this time something else was happening.

Mace was bound to a chair by clasps. Nearby two men sat, wearing the loose flowing garments associated with the high-ranking and leisured classes. It was the apparel that had confused Boaz at first. The men did not look like policemen.

One leaned toward Mace, listening intently. And Mace was talking. It was evident she was drugged. Drugs that could get a person eagerly to tell all, on any subject, without inhibition or hint of falsehood, were legion.

"What's the range?" he asked. The answer was what he expected: just over seven miles. "Show me where."

The ship fed a route map to his brain, storing it in his adplant. Boaz wasted no time in getting ready. He pulled on his modsuit, and went to the storeroom. He selected a

135

hand gun and a cutting beamer, both of which he tucked into two of the many recesses of the suit.

He went to a cupboard, opened a flask, and drank a long draught of glucose-rich nutrient syrup.

"Get up onto the ground," he ordered the ship, "and be ready to take off when I return."

The ship robots were busying themselves when he left. He made his way to the travel agency just outside the ship ground, and dialed a small ten-booth agency whose number he had to get from the directory after consulting the map in his mind.

He emerged on a nearly deserted walkway. At his back, the blank wall of a building seemed to extend forever. Before him, on the other side of the walkway, a tangled vista of rectilinear shafts gave the usual view of the three-dimensional urban jungle that was Kathundra, interspersed with lamp-suns that relieved the gloom of the lower city and created a glowing haze.

He paused with eyes closed, waiting for the wave of sickness that ran through his body to fade. Then he turned left and walked along the wall until coming to the entrance he knew would be there.

The huge blank-walled building was multifunctional. In it were several thousand dwellings, businesses, workshops, private clubs, dens and enterprises of all sorts, slotted into a mazelike inner structure. What they all had in common was a measure of secrecy. The building had no internal addresses, and all its force-transport numbers were unlisted. The only way to find any of the apartments was to be given a travel number or already to know the way there. For such privacy, the rentees paid highly.

But it was no protection against Joachim Boaz. He moved into the lobby, which was a long tunnel, square in cross-section, the wells roughened and grey and punctuated with elevator gates and the openings of flow-corridors. A tomblike quiet prevailed. The air was dead and oppressive.

Along the flowing floors of silent corridors, down in silently running elevators, Boaz came to a grey, numberless door. He took out the cutting beamer and began to trace out a rough square around the lock.

The tool's nearly invisible radiation blade, carrying very

little heat but maximum penetrating power, sliced into the metal. The main difficulty with a cutting beam was that the shear line was so thin that metals tended to bond themselves back together after the beam had passed. To prevent this Boaz placed a sucker pad against the section and jiggled it slightly until, the cutting complete, it came away altogether.

He knew that an alarm would go off as the door opened. Beyond it was an empty room. He crossed it at a run, and almost without losing momentum smashed into a second door with a booted foot and a fist.

The plastic panel shattered under the impact of his ship-enhanced strength. Kicking his way through the fragments, he emerged into the second room, putting away the cutting beam and taking out his hand gun.

During his long years of dependence on his ship Boaz had become used to foreknowledge. He already knew what he would find in the room. The interrogation was over. Mace, still held by clasps, lolled in the chair. The two robed men, who moments before had been sitting pensively, had risen at the sound of the alarm and now stared at Boaz with a lack of reaction that was curious until one realized that, after all, there was little they could do about what was happening. Boaz blocked the only exit. Neither man was armed. Usually, people in the addressless building saw little need for protection other than simply being there.

The taller of the two was a man with blue eyes that were clear and direct. With raised eyebrows, he coolly appraised the intruder.

"Captain Joachim Boaz, I presume?" he said after a moment's hesitation.

"How do you know me?" Boaz asked gruffly.

"You look the part, Captain. I admit, I had not anticipated that you would turn up here. You are even more resourceful than I had thought."

Boaz used his gun to wave both men to the rear of the room. The use of the archaism "Captain" in place of "shipkeeper" disconcerted him slightly. He stepped to Mace, taking hold of her face in a thick hand and directing her eyes to him. She stared up without recognition.

He released the clamps on her wrists and waist. "Stand

up," he ordered. When she did not respond he hauled her to her feet. Unsteadily she stayed on her feet, leaning on his shoulder. He backed away, guiding her toward the door, keeping the gun trained on her interrogators.

"Stop," the taller man said.

Boaz's plan was to leave by the transport cubicle he had seen in the other room. Regretfully he was thinking to himself that he would have to kill these two first. But he halted.

Something in the situation was odd.

Apart from the lack of formal dress, apart from the furtive location, there was the behavior between the two men. The smaller individual with sandy hair and a snub nose had said nothing and seemed unready to take any initiative, looking to the other as a disciple toward a master.

Boaz recognized that look. It was a feature of many philosophic or occult groups, whose members were apt to fall into what Madrigo had termed thelemic transfer—the surrender of the individual's personal will to the superiors in the order.

"I take it you are government?" he queried.

"Yes and no. Let me introduce myself. I am Cere Chai Hebron, Director of the Department of Scientific Affairs. My friend here—" he indicated the other—"also works for the government. But today neither of us is acting in an official capacity. We are, to put it bluntly, committing a crime, as you are."

He smiled, without mirth but in an apparent attempt to win Boaz's confidence. "I think you should listen to me. Without my help you stand little chance of leaving Kathundra alive. You see, it is not simply a matter of illegal possession of alien artifacts. I am sure you have little idea of the alarm with which the government regards your very existence, or of the effort that is being put into tracking you down."

A bundle of questions arose in Boaz's mind. In particular he wondered how these people had found Mace. But then it occurred to him that this man Hebron, if that was his real name, could be doing nothing more than feeding him information gained from Mace herself. Perhaps she was the victim of a random kidnapping, snatched to satisfy the festering lusts or warped hobbies of pleasure-sated

Kathundrans. The man was evidently trying to delay him, and every extra moment spent here increased his danger.

He started back again. "At least let me call Aban Ebarak here to talk to you," Hebron said hurriedly.

Again Boaz stopped. That name could not have come from Mace.

"You know Ebarak?"

"Indeed. You and I are collaborators, in a way."

"What is his number?"

Hebron recited a string of digits, which Boaz matched against the number he held in his adplant. He nodded, but was still suspicious. "Come here," he said.

Beckoning them into the other room, he dialed. After a short wait Ebarak appeared on the vision plate by the side of the booth which was inset into the wall. Boaz pushed Hebron before it.

"Do you know this man?"

Guardedly Ebarak nodded. "Yes. He's a Cabal Director."

"What can I expect from him?"

Ebarak, reluctant to say anything incriminating over a public service, looked ill at ease. "You could say he's on our side," he murmured eventually.

"Then we're coming through. Stand by."

"I was suggesting Aban come *here*," Hebron said diffidently.

"Get in the booth, both of you."

Still at gunpoint, they obeyed. After dispatching them Boaz dialed again, pulled Mace in after him, and stepped out with her in Ebarak's vestibule.

Only the scientist was present. "They've gone into the lounge," he said. "You will join us?"

"They gave Mace a truth drug. Bring her round for me."

"Bring her in here."

He led Boaz into the laboratory and helped him lower Mace into a chair. Disappearing into a storeroom, he returned a few moments later with a hypodermic into which he measured a tiny amount of colorless fluid.

With a faint hiss the drug went into Mace's bloodstream. "She'll be all right. Don't suppose he gave her anything to hurt her, anyway."

"Do you mind telling me what this is all about?"

Ebarak smiled wryly. "Philosophy again. A human preoccupation that seems capable of producing an endless variety of fanatics."

"I had guessed it," Boaz muttered.

Mace seemed to have fallen asleep. Ebarak arranged her limbs more comfortably in the deep armchair. "You see, the government, including the Cabal itself, has unwittingly become host to a secret occult society, and its beliefs are treasonable. Cere Hebron, the tall fellow in the next room, is Director of this society. He is also Director of the Department of Scientific Affairs." He shrugged. "I haven't been able to tell you this before, but we have both, to some extent, been under his protection. I have also been obliged to collaborate with his society in the matter of research into the time-gems."

"These treasonable beliefs concern time?" Boaz asked.

"Yes. The society's aims are broadly speaking the same as your own. But the philosophical background is quite different."

Unseen by Ebarak, Cere Chai Hebron had slipped into the laboratory while he spoke. "That is right, Captain Boaz," he said quietly. "And yet you, I gather, should be able to appreciate that background."

"What 'philosophy' is it that makes it necessary to kidnap an innocent woman?" Boaz demanded brusquely.

"I make no apology," Hebron replied, unperturbed. "The Great Work is of such magnitude that any act committed in pursuit of it is praiseworthy. As it is, I took your friend so as to gain an insight into your good self, Captain. And I am glad that I did."

He moved closer, without a glance at Mace. His gaze on Boaz was open and disconcerting. "Listen closely, and I will explain our doctrine. We reject the colonnader teaching on the absoluteness of mind-fire. We believe it is not a state of ultimate consciousness, but only a kind of limpid sleep, a clear, calm quiescence. The whole universe is in this state of quiescence, whether in its latent or its manifest phase. Essentially, it consists of the fact that nothing ever changes. The Mirror Theorem proves this. It is what we call predestination. But what does predestination signify? To those of us in the society it merely signifies that existence has not yet evolved true consciousness and will. What consciousness does exist, either as pure mind-fire or as the smaller consciousness that is present in every one of us, is passive and not in command of itself.

"In this condition, the universe resembles a flower, or some other plant, that blossoms by day and closes up by night, and does nothing more. This opening and closing, of course, symbolizes the manifest and latent stages of the world. So it has been for no one knows how long.

"But it will not remain so forever. The universe is capable of further development. There is a higher destiny—to evolve a new, more intense consciousness that is not quiescent, but which instead is capable of change and innovation. Only creatures possessing individual consciousness can take this step, and doubtless this is the reason why such creatures—organic creatures—exist. We believe it is man's specific duty to generate the new consciousness. We are the acme of creation. But we are still conditioned by the material universe. We can, if we choose, become its masters."

Boaz turned his face away. It was no wonder Hebron was interested in him, he thought. He remembered Gare Romrey. It was more than likely he had disclosed Boaz's quest under interrogation.

"You see how closely our ambitions match, Captain," Hebron went on. "The difference is that you seek only escape. You have not grasped that the goal is rather a glorious new adventure. To create wholly new events! To control time, space and materiality!" His eyes shone. "To become, in a word, *gods*. That is our future—a future outside the dead time we are used to.

"And yet if anyone has earned a place in our society, it is you, Captain," Hebron added calmly. "You see, I have learned all about you from your girl. On Meirjain you met the ibis-headed man, who told you the secret of attaining super-consciousness." He gestured. "All this technical research is unnecessary. The secret is in the *will*. If you can descend into hell, and emerge unbroken, you will become a god."

"Except that no one could do it," Boaz said bitterly.

"Not even if it is the *only* way? Think, Boaz. We are a madcap species. Some man, somewhere, must brave that which cannot be faced. Perhaps it will be our society that implements the ibis-headed man's instructions."

"You will not implement it. If you try, you will fail. You could not endure that agony. I could not. No one can, and if either your aim or mine depends on it the cause is lost."

"In any case," he said after a pause, "are you not guilty of a failure of perspective? The universe has spawned millions of species, any of whom might be candidates for this transformation you speak of. More likely than ourselves, for instance, might be the ibis-headed people."

Hebron laughed. "Have you not committed the same hubris, Captain? Why should *you* be the only mite who can move a mountain? Yet that has not deterred you. We believe that man *is* unique. Time and again it has been shown that other races, while they may be advanced intellectually, lack man's daring. The ibis-headed man tried to denigrate this forceful quality of ours by calling it obsessiveness. Yet because of it, our guess is that it is man's destiny to be the inheritor of the new universe. Look!"

Suddenly he held up his open hand, palm outward. He seemed to concentrate for a moment or two, and on the pale palm words appeared, standing out blood-red:

WHO
DARES
WINS

"Our identifying motto. A willed stigma, made visible by mental effort. You may bear this stigma, if you choose."

"I take it *you* do not adhere to this doctrine?" Boaz said to Ebarak.

Ebarak's wry smile returned. "I'm a scientist," he said. He rapped his knuckles on the workbench, producing a hollow drumming sound. "Matter and force are what are real, not ideas. As for belief without proof, I've no time for that."

Hebron waved his hand, allowing the motto to fade. "Aban's is a shallow attitude. Science rests on philosophical thought; it is nothing without it. Your own mentor pointed that out to me, Captain. But I detect, somehow, that you are not with us."

"That's right," Boaz said. He did not like the look of Hebron, or the sound of his philosophical society, which he sensed was ruthlessness personified. "Your teaching is interesting, but my aims are purely negative. I don't care about the future of existence, on whatever plane."

Hebron gave no sign of disappointment. "We are bound to work together, nevertheless." He turned to Ebarak. "I was going to contact you today anyway. Orm is on the point of tracking down Captain Boaz. He may well discover his connection with you, too. I can't delay matters long—you had both better get out. Best, in fact, if we move the whole operation to a fringe planet I have selected." He turned back to Boaz. "Gems, equipment and most of the staff will leave by separate ships in separate directions. You leave first. You can join up with us later."

"And why should I allow *you* to dictate my actions?" Boaz responded in an unfriendly tone.

The Director smiled. "Can you be so ignorant? Are you unaware of *why* time research is banned? It is because whatever Aban may say about it, government scientists *do* think that time mutation is possible. The Cabal is a traditionalist institution, just like any government anywhere. In its eyes time research threatens destruction. So if I tell you that the Rectification Branch has orders to hunt you down with unusual vigor, you will realize that you took an enormous risk in coming here. Perhaps I will return to my office today and be informed that your ship has already been traced to Kathundra. For a few hours I can delay its seizure, but no more. So do as I say, take your girl and go where I tell you—before it is too late."

The news startled Boaz. It made him feel vulnerable, reminding him that the surrounding city was, in effect, hostile territory—and that he was miles from his ship, linked to it only by its subtle beams. Could these alone be enough to break his cover? Until now he had not thought so. He had presumed that the government of the decaying econosphere would not have the latest technical refinements in its armory, and that the integrator beams would remain invisible. But then he had taken only routine methods of surveillance into account. . . .

He found it bewildering that the totally private nature of his mission to change time should have been breached.

That other minds considered it valid, that it was a secret political issue, made the concept seem paradoxically unreal. He doubted, too, that he had any real friends here. Hebron's cooperative attitude was probably connected with the fact that Boaz still had a hoard of time-gems in his possession.

Mace stirred, opened her eyes abruptly and stared about her in alarm.

Boaz placed a reassuring hand on her shoulder. "All right," he said, speaking to Hebron, "we'll do as you say."

Chapter
TEN

Again, lemon-sherbet skies. Again, sitting on a hill to contemplate a fading universe.

Except that it was a different hill, and a different town sprawling below it. Except that this time Mace was beside him, and that his thoughts and feelings were, comparatively, confused.

"You took a long time getting here," she said.

"I made a mistake," he told her. "I stopped over at Al-Kadron to buy fuel rods. I was spotted by Rectification Branch agents. I had to kill three of them."

It was soon after leaving Kathundra that he had parted company with Mace, feeling that the risk of capture was too great and should not involve her. But she had insisted on a rendezvous. When he arrived on Chaunce, the planet chosen by Hebron, it was to find her waiting.

His delayed, wandering course—he had taken eight standard months in getting here—was not entirely due to caution. In a deeper sense, Boaz had lost his way. Now, when he should at last have been feeling some hope of success in his mission, it was as if the quest itself had deserted him, and the iron-hard certainty in his soul seemed, despite himself, to waver, and all his efforts to seem trivial and useless.

"I think Hebron is here," Mace told him.

He looked at her in surprise. "What makes you think that?"

"Ebarak was acting shifty the last time I saw him, and

there were some official people about. I got the idea Hebron had arrived to see how the research was going. Ebarak wouldn't tell me that, of course."

Boaz grunted. He had already seen Ebarak himself, and the scientist had said nothing of this.

Hebron was probably disappointed in Ebarak's results so far. Scientifically, they were exciting—but they came nowhere near satisfying the exalted ambitions of the Director and his group.

"They've created a new future-myth," Boaz murmured. "The myth of an operator-controlled universe, with man as the operator." He shook his head. "Men as the new gods of a new universe. What an absurd notion. Anthropomorphism carried to the ultimate degree. It's the best piece of squirreling I've heard."

"Squirreling?"

"Sorry." Mace would not know the word; it was a technical term of obscure derivation. "Losing sane perspective. Going nuts." His words sounded despairing. "What I mean is, in my view Hebron's crew are barely sane, and probably actually deranged. It's a ludicrous spectacle."

Mace began to laugh, unpleasantly, mockingly. It startled him, and he turned to her, disconcerted.

"You're some alec, Joachim. You see derangement clearly in their case, but you're incapable of seeing the same thing in yourself. It's comic!"

"What are you saying?"

"Well, isn't your objective the same as theirs, basically, and just as egocentric? I agree, they are mad. But by the same token so must you be."

"It was never conceivable that you could understand me," Boaz said, averting his face again, and feeling disappointed at her lack of sympathy.

"Why not? Because I'm uneducated? Just the same, I'm a *bonewoman*, remember." She stood up and moved in front of him, brashly confronting him. Her big breasts fell bulkily in her shift as she leaned toward him. Her face was annoyed and admonishing. "Why don't you just *drop* it? Why don't you stop pitying yourself? There's still time left to *live!*"

"Live? It is living that's the trouble." Boaz's voice sounded burdened. He didn't know why he was again taking the trouble to explain himself to her. It was the first time since his childhood that anyone's derision had affected him. "As you said, you have no proper education in philosophy. For that reason you don't quite comprehend that an unbearable past is to be feared—because it is also the future."

"Here we go again." Mace waved her hand. "Philosophy's all junk, do you hear me? *Junk:* How do you *know* the past repeats itself? It's only a theory. It's only what people *think.* Perhaps the world *doesn't* repeat itself the way you say it does. Perhaps it just goes on and on forever, changing all the time."

"It's been scientifically proved."

To Boaz's vast surprise Mace uttered a sound of disgust and kicked him as hard as she could in the shin. "If you could list everything that's been 'scientifically proved' and still turned out wrong, it would make the world's longest book. All the scientists do is play around with ideas they got from philosophers. Some deep-thinking alec says, 'the world is made of lemons and bananas.' So the scientists get busy and start calculating, until they come up with some 'equation' that tells you how many lemons and how many bananas there are. Fifteen million lemons and nineteen million bananas, or something. And there's your proof. What fools you people are."

Boaz did not look up. One part of him dismissed what Mace was saying as shallow ignorance. But another part of him, the part that had felt shaken and uneasy over recent months, saw in it an unfamiliar viewpoint that jolted his perception of things.

How did he know? How could he be *certain* that cosmic recurrence was true? How could anyone?

Could a bacterium, however hard it tried, ever chart the cycles of cosmic evolution?

Surveying the town below, he recalled that other occasion when he had noted how the econosphere's fading glory seemed, in the human imagination, to invest the universe itself with an aura of nostalgia—a subjective impression that could only be delusory, given the span of cosmic life. By the same token, was not the whole scope of human thought also inapplicable to the universal immensity? Against that immensity, was not any idea, however trivial and shallow, like the seedy charm of the town below? It was a novel thought, a shocking thought, but suddenly he could not understand why it had never occurred to him that behind all the teachings of Madrigo, so steeped in ataraxy, so rational, so wise—a rock of sanity, a paragon of the intellect—there might lurk a single ineradicable fact of human knowledge: that no one knew anything.

If the colonnaders were wrong, his burden was lifted. A surge of joy jolted through him at the prospect. Free of fear! Free of return to pain! Free to live, and then to live no more!

How was it that Mace's harsh, uneducated words could, in the space of moments, rip open his garment of decades of stubborn brooding? No, it could not be . . . an ignorant, suicidal girl could not know better than Madrigo. . . .

He became aware that, unknown to himself, he had taken his colonnader cards from his pocket and was sifting them idly through his hands. He glanced down, faced with the appalling new impression that these superb, numinous symbols were after all pure invention. . . . Then Mace snatched them from him and flung them away. He saw them go fluttering over the cyan grass of the hilltop.

Next, she swiftly unfastened her shift and let it fall from her body, revealing her nakedness. He saw from the exalted, ecstatic look in her eye that she was switching on her bone functions one by one. She leaned close to him, her hands resting on his shoulders, the aroma of her rising from her body, her plump, firm breasts, nipples erect, filling his vision.

"Forget it all, Joachim," she hissed. "Remember you are a boneman. Come on! Switch on your bones! Feel them glowing within you!"

He sat motionless, not responding. She placed her cheek against his. "Philosophy isn't real. But what bones give you, *that's* real. Ever since it happened, you haven't allowed yourself anything good, Joachim. That's the trouble. You must learn to *enjoy*. That's the only way to wipe out the past."

Boaz, his picture of himself and the world, were all adrift. At present he had no sexual feeling. But to Mace's cajoling he answered at last by dredging from his memory the all-but-forgotten controlling syllables.

It was like remembering flavors lost in the past. *Felicity* came on: for the first time in many years he knew the joy of emotion and sensation linked together, of delight at the sight of his surroundings, at sounds and smells, at the sigh of air on his skin. *Adjusted rheobase* came on, and everything he perceived became sharper and more vivid than an unboned man would have thought possible. *Adjusted chronaxy* slowed his time sense. Mace, as she edged closer to him, was performing a vast balletic dance in which every slight movement, every pore of her skin, took part.

At her urging whisper, the sex function came on.

She was helping him out of his modsuit, out of the sheathlike undergarment. "Higher," she moaned. "Take it all the way. You can stand it."

Her hands ran over his ravaged skin. He obeyed her, pushing all the settings higher and higher, to maximum, until his mind dizzied with the assault of impressions and sensations, and the aid of the ship was necessary to maintain his sanity.

Oh, it was madness! It was a seething cauldron of desire, a world of endless eroticism, a delirium of delight that snatched away his identity and put in place of it— pleasure! Infinite excitement! She grappled with him until they scarcely knew which was which, and in a dazzling flashing fog of arousal he felt his ship, visible on the level ground to one side of the town, gearing itself up, getting ready to raise his phallus—which he would not have been able to do without its help, although it had never been called upon to accomplish this for him before.

A hard, bulky object filled his being, a tower of strength. Then—penetration. Now it filled her being too, dominant, lunging.

Into fire. Into a burning, seething, hopeful world.

The light gravity of Chaunce made Cere Chai Hebron feel slightly unsteady. To increase his weight marginally he wore a slimmed modsuit, scarcely more bulky than a chemise and hose, but this too lacked comfort. He liked his raiment to be loose and flowing.

But for the news of Boaz's arrival he would have re-

turned to Kathundra by now. "That is his ship, you say?"
he said. He pointed through the recessed upper-story window, over the roofs of the town to the space vessel that
distinguished itself by its tall, rounded form among the
more ungainly shapes on the ship ground.

"Yes, Grand Master. That is his ship."

A dozen members of *Thelema*, seated in formal conven-
tion, faced Grand Master Hebron. Nine of them had been
hastily summoned from Kathundra and had arrived only
that morning. Hebron turned from the window and
resumed his seat, twirling the toga he wore over his modsuit around him.

"Those of us who came earlier," he said, "have evalu-
ated the work carried out by Citizen Ebarak and our own
scientists on the time artifacts." He hesitated. "Our scientists have not been called to this meeting, for tactical reasons. It is best that what I have to tell you should not
reach the ears of Ebarak.

"The results are disappointing. It is unlikely that the
time-gems will be of any help in achieving our aims. But
then, I had reached this conclusion even before the work
was moved to Chaunce. As you know, we have gained
new information. Through suffering, the mind of man may
become the mind of a god."

Not a hint of reaction came from his followers (all
men—women were not permitted into the higher ranks of
Thelema) as he reminded them of the nature of their
quest. Their discipline, which included restraint in the expression of feeling, was good. "The secret lies, then, not in
some technical resource, but in the strength of our own
will. But can suffering of the requisite intensity be mastered? It must of necessity be transcendent and therefore
unendurable. One individual *has* known this degree of suffering, but failed to be transformed: the shipkeeper
Joachim Boaz, a strange man who was marked ineradica-
bly by his experience."

He paused for almost ten seconds, then in the growing
silence said: "It is true to say that Boaz is not really a
man at all. His body is incapable of sustaining its own life.
It is dependent on adp machinery within his ship, which
integrates his every somatic function over a communica-

tion beam. The ship, rather than the walking man, is the bodily Boaz."

He again indicated the window, in which Boaz's ship, not far away on the ship ground, was neatly framed. Hebron did not know that at that moment it was assisting Boaz in an ecstasy of a wholly positive nature. "We have a unique opportunity for researching the true means to attaining transcendental consciousness. Control that ship, and we control Boaz. That gives us the means to use him as an experimental subject. It is said that the alien being on Meirjain offered to reintroduce Boaz to his agony, so he could attempt to overcome it. Though he did not have the courage to accept, we can force the issue on him, again and again if need be. Since he failed the test once he will do so again; but in so doing he will provide us with valuable data. This is indispensable if we are to prepare ourselves for the same trial."

Hebron stopped, looking the meeting over in the manner that tacitly allowed questions. "Why should this particular individual be valuable to us?" someone asked.

"For two reasons: he is uniquely controllable, and he has already been close to the transcendental state. He is a natural subject for research into it."

"And what if our manipulations should, after all, cause him to cross the barrier?" someone else asked. "Our position might be unenviable."

Hebron smiled. "We are playing with fire," he agreed. "Mind-fire, to be exact. Anyone who is afraid has no place in *Thelema*."

He nodded to one nearest him, who then read out a list of names from among those newly arrived from Kathundra: the attack team.

"Our task is simple," Hebron told them. "You will break into the Boaz ship and gain control over the equipment there, using the apparatus you brought with you. You must analyze it before he can return to confront you—he is a fierce adversary if opposed. Once you succeed, he can do nothing by himself."

The small man who had helped Hebron with the interrogation of Mace spoke. "Is there not a moral issue here?"

"Why should there be?" Hebron said, his tone supercilious. "Who will judge a god?"

In another part of the town (which was much like Hondora, the town Boaz had been thinking of a few minutes earlier) a smaller meeting took place. The Rectification Branch colonel had not arrived on Chaunce in uniform but he donned it now, feeling more secure, stronger, in the shiny black and green, in the broad utensil belt and slant hat.

The room was small and low-ceilinged, shielded against every known spy-ray. Every police station in the econosphere had such a room. "It is confirmed, then," he said to the three non-uniformed agents with him. "The quarry is here."

"He is here, sir." The agents, though large of build, had an anonymous blankness about them. They were selected for it: it was supposed to make their activities more invisible. The colonel wasn't sure if the ploy wasn't sometimes counterproductive: put several of them together, and their ordinariness became almost glaring.

"This is a matter of importance," he said. "I can tell you that I have come straight from the Chief. Orm's orders are that Boaz is to be liquidated outright. No attempt at arrest."

"There are problems in either case, sir."

"Yes . . . he is a difficult man to stop. If we were in Kathundra, now, it would be different." He chuckled. The police in Kathundra had a secret right of control over the force-transport network. Any citizen under observation could, at any time he entered a travel booth, be switched straight to a police cell or killing chamber, or even circulated endlessly through the system for as long as need be. . . . "But there is an easier way," he went on. "This creature Boaz has a grave deficiency. He is a man on remote: his ship keeps him alive. To destroy him, one should destroy his ship, preferably choosing a time when the two are separated. . . ."

They spoke further, laying plans and appointing a time. In actual fact the plotting of Boaz's course had been firming up for more than a standard month: that Chaunce would be his final destination had been extrapolated in advance. Police Chief Orm had gleefully told the colonel an even more interesting fact: Chaunce had a secret visitor, a government minister no less, though Orm was not at liberty to name him. Nevertheless when he made his report it would be to the full Cabal, and someone very important had better have a damned good explanation. . . . Treason in high places was a crime for which Police Chief Orm had particular relish.

Chapter

ELEVEN

No longer was Boaz fighting a figment. For the first time, perhaps, since he had wakened in the city of Theta with a new, straight skeleton, with silicon bones that promised a new future, he knew a measure of happiness.

He was in a fun room with Mace, just off the main arcade of the sprawling, blossom-smelling town. The room itself was a work of art: walls a delicate shade of yellow, embossed with a frieze which could give the occupants enough suggestions to last a week; carpeted and furnished with a softness that made it seem a playland. An ever-changing spectrum of perfumes made the air continually fresh and pleasant. Subliminal sounds—inaudible to those whose senses were not heightened by silicon bones—fed one's sense of well being with constant, encouraging music.

They had rested, and now were ready to begin again. Mace smiled, and touched his naked shoulder. "Your body has qualities," she said, "that are yours alone."

He looked down at his craggy self. She did not mention that perpetual virility was one of them: that was not unique—it was available by a simple piece of surgery. More important to him, in any case, was the new virility that had come to his mind.

That dreadful past, of course, was still there. But he could now bring himself to have the memory erased if he wished, flushed from his psyche. In fact, he had decided not to. Mace had shown him another way, another goal.

154

He would seek pleasure the equal of that pain! Even now he could not help but put it in philosophical terms. In the colonnader cards the principle of justice, or equilibrium, was all important. If such a principle truly existed in the universe, then his agony *must* be balanced by an equal *positive* experience able to cancel its evil effects!

He had not mentioned this piece of reasoning to Mace. She would only have laughed. It was a wonder to him, a marvel, that all she had done was to open his eyes to what any untutored workman, nymphgirl or shopkeeper could have told him—that because a body of ideas was impressive, and had the backing of civilization and classical discourse, did not make it true.

She opened her palm. In it rested four little filter plugs, two pink, two pale blue. "The blue ones are for men," she said. "Put them in."

He took them and, following her example, inserted them in his nostrils. "Now we spray each other," she said. "Remember to breathe through your nose."

She handed him a blue spray-gun that she took from a cushion, taking a pink one herself. Her selective nose filters protected her from the highly charged male-directed pheromonic molecules she puffed at him; his kept out the female-directed chemicals he puffed at her.

Standing only a couple of feet apart, they drenched each other. She threw back her head as she silently set her bone functions. She tossed aside the spray-gun, discarded the nose filters. She threw open her arms.

"Bones!" she screeched quietly. "Your bones, Boaz!"

Excitedly, he began to raise, and raise yet higher.

The low, single sun was casting long probing fingers across the ship ground when three large men, wearing the garb of technicians, approached an unusually upright cargo ship. They paused at the bottom of the tread-rail. Then one stepped on, his hand inside his tunic, holding the stock of the heat-and-shock pistol with which to force the hatch. As the rail started to flow the others stepped on after him, ready with hand weapons to deal with any defensive robots, the last man carrying the case of thermal grenades.

At the top, he received a surprise.

The hatch lock was already blown.

He signed the others to be cautious, then eased the hatch open and stepped through, placing his feet with cat-like quietness. He was on a between-decks gallery. A ship robot lay on the floor, limbs awry. It had a blast hole through its chest.

The others followed him in. "Someone's been here before us," he murmured. "They could still be on board."

"Probably common robbers."

"Then they can go with the rest of it. Come on."

Their main job was to make sure they blew both the transmitter and the processors. But this was a custom-built ship; it had not been possible to obtain a design print. He went through a door at the end of the gallery and found himself on a deck that was, he guessed, over the hold.

His eyes quickly adjusted to the dim light. The deck had a crammed appearance. It seemed to be made up of corridors whose walls were dull-colored casings that whirred and clicked. On each casing was a dully glowing green check screen, so that the whole deck was filled with the eerie luminescence—the only light there was, apparently.

At the end of the first corridor two men, clad in black cat-suits, knelt by a flat box shape. Part of a casing had been cut away, and the innards connected to the box by adp-fibers. The nearby green screen was oscillating wildly.

"Police," the Rectification Branch man announced in a cold voice. "On your feet, keep your hands in sight."

The two jumped up, eyes flicking from the pale, undistinguishable faces of the Branch men to the guns they held. "We are on official business," said one.

"Whose?"

There was no answer. Though incurious as to the truth of the claim, the Branch man was slightly mollified. "Get out fast," he said. "This ship is to be destroyed."

The other's eyes widened in alarm. "No! It's ours! It has to be preserved—"

There came a noise from behind the casing. Another cat-suited figure came around the bend of the corridor. This one was armed with a force gun.

The Branch men did not wait. Two of them opened fire. The unarmed victims before them cried out in panic and cringed, flinging out their arms in a useless, self-defensive reflex. WHO DARES WINS glared briefly on the palms of their hands, before they fell.

The third Branch man did not see the stigmata. He was crouched down between two casings and was opening his box of thermal grenades.

Mace was anointing his body with oil when Boaz first began to feel prodromic flashes of discomfort.

His bone settings were high, so high it was as if he were transported to another world. Yet it was a world in which Mace was present with him, into which they had entered together. In that world she had said to him: this is the future for mankind. We are like a new species, we bone people. Others cannot understand it. Hebron, Ebarak, they do not have bones. You can tell it. Everything about them is dull.

And, yes, it was true. It was true that new powers glowed within one, that the world was transfigured. That those without bones were to be pitied.

He moved a foot or two away from her, trying to identify the new source of physical unease.

Then unseen fire suddenly enveloped him, moving in a flash from the soles of his feet to the crown of his head. His ship screamed to him, one last cataclysmic message.

COLLAPSE

He knew in an instant that nothing could save him. He had failed to evade the Rectification Branch. His ship was being destroyed. All the work of the bonemakers, whose skill and resource had made of him again a functioning human entity, was being undone piece by piece as the regulating departments of the ship went out one by one. He took a step forward, and seemed, howling, to move as through a crystal lattice of pain. Too late, he realized he had unthinkingly keyed in *all* his bone functions, including—just as on that far-off day on the edge of the alchemists' firepit—the preservation function. Too late, he realized he no longer had the power to switch any of them off.

The difference was that this time all the functions were on setting eight. The agony mounted and mounted, and mounted and mounted, fed by the super-senses silicon bones insisted, still, on giving him. He was back there. He was back with what he feared most, back in the pit, and Boaz howled his rage, howled his fear, screamed and screeched with his efforts to escape, to evade, to overcome, in any way at all to come to terms with torment as his bleak, twisted soul knew again its aloneness and its damnation. For the bones took that pain, took it, delighted in it, presented it to him enhanced to the ultimate. He journeyed a million years through winding labyrinths of exquisite, ecstatic agony. He dwelt in palaces of pain, he inhabited cities and civilizations based on the technology of torture.

And in that pain, as hellish super-fire whirled for the second time through his being, Boaz remembered. *He remembered*. With a depth of recall impossible to mistake, he remembered this scene. He had lived it before. A thousand, a million times before. He remembered how he died, minutes from now, thrashing about the room and killing Mace in his uncontrolled spasms.

With that, he stopped screaming, though he felt system after system collapse within him as the somatic disaster deepened. He tried to speak, and words came out, the voice roaring, distorted, from a furnace of suffering.

"The—colonnaders—are—right. . . . The—world—repeats. . . ."

Hand to mouth, eyes wide, she stared at him in horror.

"But—death—is—not—an—end—to—be—sought, Mace. . . . Go—escape—live!"

He turned from her. "It need not be!"

He went crashing through the flimsy wall of the fun room. He staggered into the dusty arcade. It was deserted, fading into a dusk relieved only by a white glare beyond the low buildings.

This prospect was new. Never in all the infinity of ages had his eyes, at this instant, beheld it.

The ship, even while dying, still fought to preserve him. He knew the Rectification agents would not be content with killing him. They would search the town, find and kill Mace too, unless he gave her a breathing space. He moved down the arcade. He staggered up an alley, smashed through a wall, and was on the ship ground.

His ship was a streaming tree of withering white fire. The first flash he had felt, from bottom to top, had been the thermal grenades exploding and taking hold even on metal. A knot of men, three with guns covering two others, stood nearer to him, using their arms to shield their faces from the heat.

There was still strength in him. He leaped to them. His eerie, screeching voice seemed to fall from the sky.

"I—Joachim Boaz—have—altered—the world. . . . Never—again—will—you—destroy—me—"

His sense of liberty was absolute. He was transgressing physical law. He had stepped out from under Nature. Their terror did not register with him as he fell on them. Three he certainly killed, two more perhaps, but then his consciousness was cut off from the outside world. A series of images passed through his mind: Priestess, Vehicle, Justice, Strength, all the colonnader cards flashing by in sequence. Then he heard an immense trumpet blast that wiped out everything. Then nothing.

10th Year as the SF Leader!
Outstanding science fiction

By John Brunner
THE WRONG END OF TIME   (#UE1598—$1.75)
THE AVENGERS OF CARRIG   (#UE1509—$1.75)
TO CONQUER CHAOS   (#UJ1596—$1.95)
THE REPAIRMEN OF
   CYCLOPS   (#UE1638—$2.25)
INTERSTELLAR EMPIRE   (#UE1668—$2.25)

By Arthur H. Landis
A WORLD CALLED CAMELOT   (#UE1418—$1.75)
CAMELOT IN ORBIT   (#UE1417—$1.75)
THE MAGICK OF CAMELOT   (#UE1623—$2.25)

By M. A. Foster
THE WARRIORS OF DAWN   (#UE1751—$2.50)
THE GAMEPLAYERS OF ZAN   (#UE1497—$2.25)
THE DAY OF THE KLESH   (#UE1514—$2.25)
WAVES   (#UE1569—$2.25)
THE MORPHODITE   (#UE1669—$2.75)

By Gordon R. Dickson
ANCIENT, MY ENEMY   (#UE1552—$1.75)
NONE BUT MAN   (#UE1621—$2.25)
HOUR OF THE HORDE   (#UJ1689—$1.95)
THE STAR ROAD   (#UE1711—$2.25)

By Ansen Dibell
PURSUIT OF THE SCREAMER   (#UE1580—$2.25)
CIRCLE, CRESCENT, STAR   (#UE1603—$2.25)

THE NEW AMERICAN LIBRARY, INC.,
P.O. Box 999, Bergenfield, New Jersey 07621

Please send me the DAW BOOKS I have checked above. I am enclosing
$_____ (check or money order—no currency or C.O.D.'s).
Please include the list price plus $1.00 per order to cover handling
costs.

Name _____

Address _____

City _____ State _____ Zip Code _____
Please allow at least 4 weeks for delivery